CLANCY WEEKS

ANODYNE DREAMS

Copyright ©2019 by Clancy Weeks
All rights reserved.
Published in the United States by Avalon Press.
  "Requiem in Blue and Pink" originally published in the anthology *Out of Many, One: Celebrating Diversity*, HWG Press, ©2017
  "Zombie Like Me" originally published in *Stupefying Stories #20*, ©2018
  Excerpt from *Sleepers*, Netherworld Books, ©2017
  Excerpt from *The Stone of Tantalus*, Avalon Press, ©2018

Avalon Press and its logo are trademarks of Avalon Press.

Title: Anodyne Dreams
Names: Weeks, Clancy, author
Descriptions: First edition. | : Avalon Press [2019]
Identifiers: ISBN-13: 978-1-7321220-2-4 (paperback) |
  ISBN-10: 1-7321220-2-4 (paperback) |
  ISBN-13: 978-1-7321220-3-1 (e-book) |
  ISBN-10: 1-7321220-3-1 (e-book)
Subjects: | Science Fiction. | Fantasy | Suspense Fiction.

First Paperback Edition

AVALON PRESS

CONTENTS

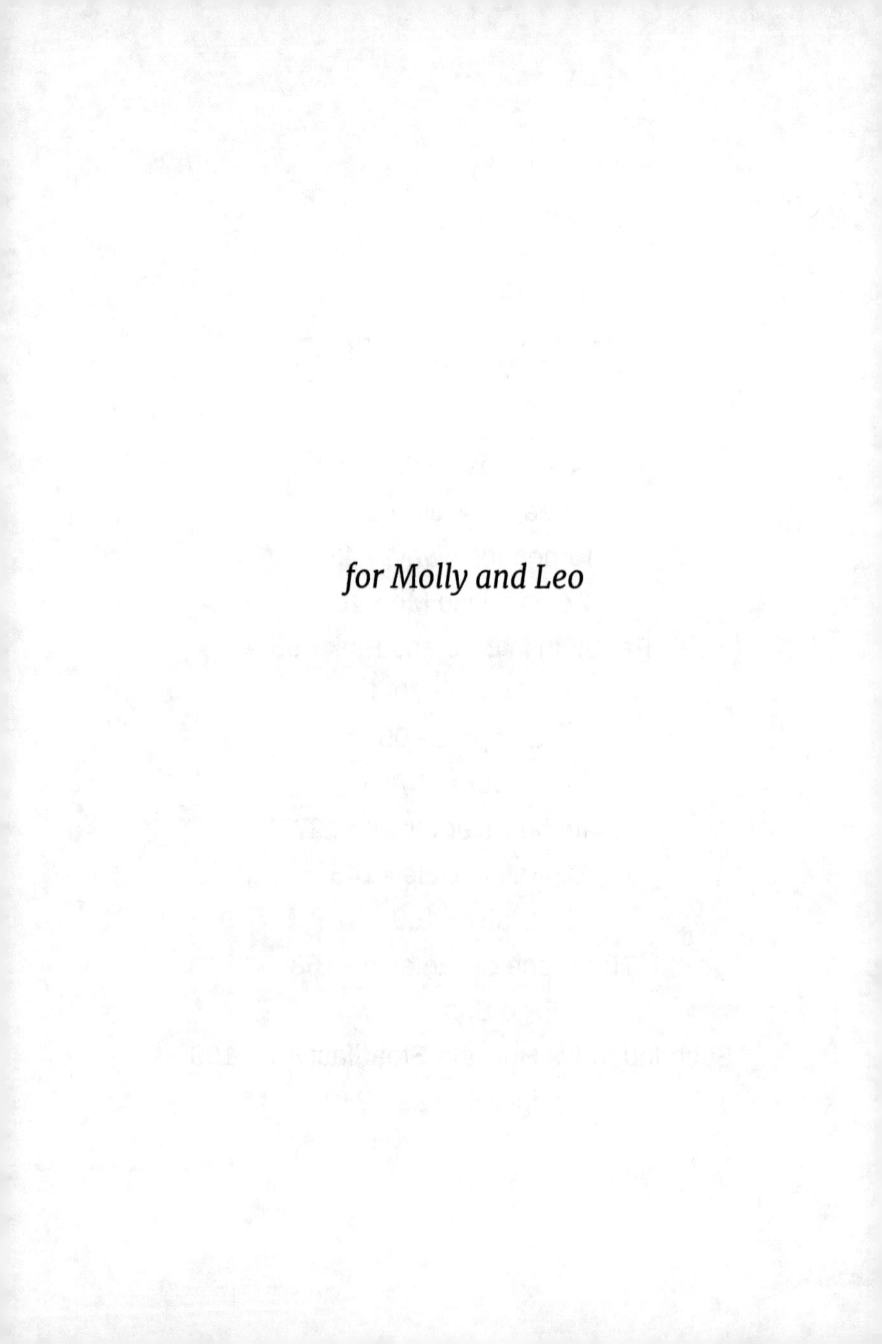

for Molly and Leo

The woods are lovely, dark and deep,
But I have promises to keep,
And miles to go before I sleep,
And miles to go before I sleep.

Some lines of prose or poetry just stick with you. These from Robert Frost's Stopping by Woods on a Snowy Evening have always been some of my favorites, and formed the kernel of this story.

...AND MILES TO GO...

"HEY, WALTER. COME LOOK AT THIS. I THINK WE'VE GOT something on HL51-8." Jordan looked up at me from his perch at the analysis station.

"Which one is that?"

"It's that weird little moon we tagged with the anomalous mass reading." He checked again to verify his numbers, "Radius of around fifty-k, and mass and surface gravity way too high for something that small."

I pulled at my beard. "I remember that thing. Almost spherical, isn't it?" Susan, my ex, hated the beard. She also hated the time I spent out on surveys, but that was my job. She especially hated the down-time with me sitting around the apartment doing a whole lot of nothing.

"That's the one." He made a small gesture with his free hand, and the little holo in his field of view changed. His eyes narrowed a bit, and he pulled on his bottom lip. "Albedo is up there too. Probably accounts for the lower than expected surface temperatures."

I don't like anomalies. Give me good old boring routine any day. It's why Susan finally gave up on us and walked out. Can't say I blame her.

I spun the useless ring on my finger. "Mark it for further study in the database. I'm ready to turn this can around and head home. This shift has already leaked into overtime, and you know how the Corps feels about that." I nodded toward the countdown clock by the main screen. "You don't want another lingering charge on our records, do you?"

He shook his head, pointedly watching me fiddle with the old wedding band. "I think we're obligated to check this out, Walt. From the numbers I'm getting here, there's a butt-load of rikenium on that little rock."

Wonderful. Element 124 was on the *confirm it now* list for decades. Normally found in very small amounts—from nuggets a millimeter in diameter all the way up to a centimeter—it was the only naturally occurring element able to create a stable Jump field. There was a pea-sized mass of the stuff right now in this very survey ship.

"Define 'butt-load,' please." I didn't relish spending time on that mobile crematorium in search of something so small, regardless of the bonus money. Our percentages were so tiny that even a larger than average haul of something as rare as rikenium would net us only a day's pay each.

He looked down at his instruments, then back up at me. "Um... the needle's pretty much pegged out here, Walt."

I'm not an optimist by nature—far from it—but the hair on the back of my neck snapped to attention at the tone of Jordan's voice.

"All right," I said, conceding defeat. "Take us down."

He gave me that huge, goofy grin of his, and barked "Brace for impact!"

He was only half kidding. I think my spine had short-ened three or four centimeters over the last year from his landings.

***

"Holy shit, Walt, it's everywhere."

For once, my shipmate wasn't exaggerating. Rikenium powder covered the surface of the little moon. Which was odd because it was usually found in small nuggets or veins in other heavy elements. Pure white, it was a snow-covered field set against a velvet night. I reached down and tried to grab a handful. Finer than talcum powder, it slid like mo-lasses through my gloves, leaving only a fine dusting. No matter how I tried, I couldn't hold more than that. It was like trying to grab a fistful of water. I never saw this form of the stuff before, and was sure no one else had, either.

"It's better than that, Jordan." I smiled in spite of my-self. "I'll bet this moon is almost completely made of the stuff." From the coring samples the powder was, so far, a uniform depth of nearly two meters before the corer stopped at something too hard to cut. Each time I pulled the tool back out, the powder slid back as if there were never a hole.

I found a solid outcropping two kilometers from the ship, and as I stood beside the boulder-sized chunk of dreams, I thought about the bonus money we'd see from this survey—and the early retirement it could buy. Hell, I can pay to retire the whole damn survey team.

"Sure, that would explain the mass readings, but how is that even possible?"

"Who cares. I'm just glad it's us and not that bastard Eugene." He was the Corps Assayer in this sector, and the reason we wandered so far from the damn ship. He was also Susan's new meal ticket, but that was the one thing I didn't hold against him. I knew the asshole would never accept the dust as verification of our find, no matter how much we brought back. The manual said rikenium came in nuggets, and nuggets it would have to be.

Jordan snorted. "Yeah, screw that guy."

Instead of chiming in on the last part, as was the station ritual, I grunted approval while I tried to figure out how to break off a chunk of the stuff. None of the tools on hand could dent it, and we hadn't the ability to smelt the powder into a solid form. The heat requirements were too high. With a plasma cutter I might lop off a section if it were thin enough, so I hopped around the boulder looking for a candidate.

"Look at how smooth it is." Jordan was on his knees, a gauntleted hand rubbing the bright silver at the edge of a large flat area nearby. "Hey," he waved at his reflection, "I can see myself!" He looked up at me with a goofy grin through the transparent bubble of his helmet.

"Cut it out, man. People will think you're not too bright." I grinned back at him. We were rich and foolishly, brilliantly, happy. That's a bad combination when you're walking on the barren surface of an airless moon.

He continued to probe the surface, leaning over the mirror finish. "I wonder what the coefficient of friction is."

"I don't think..."

"Do you think we can skate on it?" And before I could stop him, he stood up and slid out over the apparently frictionless surface. He was on the other side of a hundred meter expanse in seconds, with no more effort than stepping off the curb. He stood there waving at me while he sang, "Ladies and gentlemen, take my advice. Pull down your pants and slide on the ice."

If I could see his face, I'm sure he looked as stupid as he sounded.

"I've got a better idea... why don't you just slide on back over here? We've been on borrowed time since we passed out of the giant's shadow. Sunrise on this rock is coming, and I don't think you want to get caught outside."

"Party pooper."

Even in an exosuit, the primary would bake us alive inside our crunchy shells in under a minute. There wasn't a way to dump the excess heat fast enough. Orbiting the gas giant on the dark side, with its own radiation output, was bad enough we could spend only a couple of days, cumulatively, in EVA. Standard enviro-suits were less than useless here.

Jordan took a single sliding step onto the rikenium ice and glided smoothly across its glassy plain. He didn't step off as forcefully as the first time because his momentum died about twenty meters from the edge. When it reversed, drawing him to the center of a shallow depression, I laughed out loud.

I probably shouldn't have done that.

***

Jordan tried to push himself forward, but it was no use. There was nothing to push against. All he succeeded in doing was an amusing little dance that took him nowhere, but managed to put a smile on my face.

"I can still hop."

But, no, he couldn't. Unless he hopped straight up, bringing him no closer to the edge than before, his boots slid out from under him. Even when he managed a small amount of forward momentum that depression kept hauling his ass back.

I had to laugh. At the time, I didn't notice the way the surface deformed and rippled with each jump attempt, but I know now it must have.

"Okay, then, what's your plan?"

"Other than watching you flounder around for another twenty minutes?" I grinned broadly, knowing full well he couldn't see my face. "I was thinking I'd hike back to the ship, get a safety line, and trudge back here to pull your ass across."

"You sure there's enough time for that?" There was a slight catch in his voice. Most would have missed it.

"Sure. Sunrise isn't for another hour, and I can get there and back in less than half that." I hoped my voice sounded reassuring, but neither of us had much practice in the art.

"Okay, but when we get back this stays between you and me, right? Nothing in the report." I heard his heavy breathing over the mic as he waited for my response. Normally I would make some stupid joke, or exact some boon from him for the service, but as he stood there, a statue in pewter-colored ceramic composites, I just couldn't.

"No problem," I chucked my chin at him as if he could see me, and grinned. "I won't even tell Eugene."

"Yeah," he said quietly through a shuddering breath. "Screw that guy."

***

The safety line, a wrench tied to the end for mass, arced over the space between myself and Jordan. Halfway through its flight I saw the trajectory was off, and would miss him wide to the left by over ten meters. Once it hit the ground, it slid forward on the frictionless surface until it reached the end of its length, then snapped back on almost the same path, never passing within grasping distance of Jordan's gloves.

"Damn, Walt. You throw like my grandmother... and she's dead."

"Hey, come over here and say that," I teased, retrieving the line one slow meter at a time. If the line would only stay still when it landed, I could walk around the lake to the right and drag his end to him. With enough practice I could play it out to kill its momentum as it hit, but I was sure we didn't have the time for that. I turned toward the ship, and the computer displayed an overhead simulation of the terminator as it approached. Time was running out.

"Heh... funny, man," he said gamely, but all the humor was leached from his words before they reached his lips.

The second throw was closer, but still off target.

"Is there a chance you need glasses or something?"

"Just shut up and be ready to catch the next one."

"I know these suits aren't built to play ball in, but damn, Walt."

"I'm beginning to think you don't trust me."

He laughed once, and I saw the telltale movement in his helmet as he shook his head. "Just throw me the damn line."

This time my aim was true, and the weighted end arced lazily across the expanse. Reaching apogee, it was clear the end of the wrench would sail far over Jordan's head, but that didn't matter, as the line would still land right on top of him. That wasn't good enough for Jordan— he had seen the line snap back on itself twice before. I saw him arching backward to get a clear view overhead, then he leaned forward and bent his knees into a low crouch. Before I realized what he was doing, he launched himself straight up, and this time I did notice the way the surface beneath him deformed at the effort. The ripples, now prominent, continued until touchdown.

In one-tenth gee everything happens in slow motion, and beautiful in its way. Jordan reached the top of his leap, snagged the line, and drifted like a balloon back to the surface. I was so mesmerized I forgot to double check the line was secure on my end. It didn't matter. Jordan landed with the force you would expect from a nearly three hundred and thirty kilogram mass dropped from a height of ten meters. The suit's servos could handle that easily, but the surface of the rikenium lake could not. The mirror deformed on impact, then collapsed inward, disappearing in an explosion of powder, and opening a fissure all the way to the near shore. As Jordan fell through and out of sight, the powder from the shoreline poured like water into the hole, covering him completely. He must have fallen far beneath the surface, because when the dust settled I noticed the line was sheered off near the fissure, and the end attached to Jordan was resting serpentine on the lake a dozen meters out of reach.

***

Pacing looks stupid in an exosuit in low-gee, but I didn't care. Burning up time like we actually had it, I paced while I tried to think our way out of this.

"I can't believe I'm going to die out here in walking distance to the damn ship!" Jordan complained non-stop the whole time, and even though I couldn't blame him, it was still frustrating.

"Shut up and let me think."

"Walt, give it up. There's nothing you can do. I've tried crawling out, but the damn dust is packed too tight, and every time I make a hole it just fills up again."

"Look, all I need to do is reach this end of the line. Once I've got that, I'm pretty sure I can pull you out." I stood there, looking at that line as it lay there mocking me, and wishing I wasn't in this suit. I had a habit of pulling on my beard while I thought and not being able to do so was distracting.

"That's a no-go, my friend. From what you said, the only way to get to it is to slide out onto the ice." He took a deep breath. "Then what?"

"Running start." It was the best I could come up with. "I take a running start and snatch it as I slide to the other side."

"And what if the ice cracks again and you go under?" Sure, it was a high-risk gamble, but what else was there? Jordan chuckled, the sound an accusation. "Besides, I've seen you throw. I don't think we have time for the thirty or forty tries it'll take."

He was right, and I knew it. I was ready to suggest something else—anything else—when my computer pinged.

"Time's up, Walt."

Sunrise was only ten minutes away. Shit. Even if I got him out right now, there wasn't time to do that and make it back to the ship.

"Walt, you have to go."

"You're right." And without thinking, I ran toward the lake and launched myself into a belly-flop. I hit the ice moving faster than I expected, and the end of the line was in my hand—and then just gone before I knew it. As I spun across the ice, I saw the line and the crater falling away behind me.

"What are you doing?"

"I took a shot, okay?" There wasn't much else to say, other than, "I'm sorry. I missed."

I slid across the lake at breakneck speed and hit the far shore with enough force to bounce me a dozen meters across the vacuum-packed rikenium snow. I stood and took aim for a second go on the return trip when the emergency alarm grated through my helmet.

"And now you don't have enough time to get back to the ship," Jordan said, the sneer clear in his voice. "Way to go."

"I guess that's it, then." I sat down facing the ship and watched the terminator on my display creep closer to our salvation. "At least it'll be quick."

"Oh, that's comforting."

I sat there a couple of minutes thinking about all the money under my ass, wondering who'd end up finally finding this place. The antenna on the ship flared brilliantly into daylight as the terminator passed on its way to the cookout that was us. Creeping across the white plain, a juggernaut of pure light and hard radiation, it was less than a kilometer from the lake when Jordan keyed his mic.

"Hey! How fast is this rock turning, anyway?"

"About six kilometers an hour."

"And in the suit, how fast can we move over level ground?"

"Nearly ten." I sat up. "So I take another shot, pull you out, and we can outrun the sunrise all the way around back to the ship!"

"Check that. You turn your ass around and start running now. There's not enough time to pull me out."

"But..."

"No buts, Walt. Get your ass in gear!"

"I can..."

"There's no time! You were lucky you didn't fall through the first time."

He was right. I didn't want him to be, but he was. There was nothing to do but turn and go, and all I wanted to do was stay and keep him company. It was stupid, of course. I'd be committing suicide for no good goddamn reason.

"Run, you moron!"

Hesitation in every motion, I turned and fled, hating myself with every comical hopping step.

Shortly into my reluctant retreat, still well within range of Jordan's radio, the silence was too much for him.

"Hey, Walt?"

"Yeah?"

"How are you gonna write up the report?"

"I'll make you out a hero," I lied. We both knew everything was recorded, and once I filed the report—accurate or not—the mining ships would find out quickly enough what went down.

We were both silent for another minute as I brooded.

Jordan was the first to break that silence. "Can you promise me two things?"

"Sure... as long as it's legal, I mean."

"Try to have fun with the money, okay? I mean... well... lighten up a bit." He chuckled again. "Show Susan what she walked out on, okay?"

"Roger that." I shook my head. The man never took anything seriously. It didn't make sense that Susan chose Eugene over a guy like Jordan. She wanted more excitement in her life, but ended up trading one stiff for another. "What's the other thing?"

"Kind of goes along with the first. I just want you to rub Eugene's nose in it real good."

I laughed genuinely at that.

"Because, you know... screw that guy," he said. As if it needed saying.

A moment later I heard the crackle of static on the radio grow as the terminator approached Jordan's position. I increased my speed.

"Hey Walt... I think I'm gonna shut my radio off now."

He didn't need to tell me why. He was doing me a kindness.

"Good idea. Conserve your batteries." I choked back stillborn tears. "It was an honor working with you."

"And you." He took one last breath, and said, "Jordan out." There was a click, and I was left with nothing but static. Angry, I shut mine off, the reward an oppressive silence.

***

I stopped and took a sip of water from the nipple on the left side of my helmet, detecting the telltale metallic tang I despised. It was clear I'd used up my pure water supply and was now drinking my own processed wastewater. It wouldn't kill me, but it also meant my suit diverted some of its power to filter, distill, and sanitize my waste for consumption.

After running for sixteen hours, my computer informed me I was now over two hours ahead of the sunrise. My on-board medical system pumped me full of stims and carbs, but there's a limit the body hits you can't ignore. Sure, the suit did all the work, but my legs still moved, and no matter how hard I tried I couldn't keep the muscles from contracting in sympathy with the forced motion. My legs were cramping, and I couldn't see straight from lack of sleep.

Tonguing the control stud, my display flashed to life and showed me where I was in relation to the ship. Though drifting slightly off course, I was still in the green for my ETA. Shutting down all my non-essential systems paid off, saving enough power to reach the ship before my batteries died.

I first sat, then laid back in the rikenium snow, breathing heavily. On impulse I stretched out my arms and legs, and executed three or four jumping jacks, smiling to myself. A million years from now that snow angel would still be there, and future explorers would never know why. Jordan would have approved.

I took nourishment from the nipple on the right side of my helmet, then a sip of water from the left, set my computer to rouse me in an hour, and fell blissfully asleep.

***

I awoke with a start to the grating buzz of the emergency alarm. The computer tried to wake me earlier with a standard ping, but after several unsuccessful attempts it changed tactics. No one resisted that sound as it always presaged impending doom.

I brought up the display and shut off the offending noise. I overslept by a mere few minutes, but I saw the terminator gaining on me in the map projected onto my visor. In this race there was no prize for second place. Pulling myself up I noticed that even though my legs felt like stone, the little time I slept worked it's magic on my limbs. Well, that and the pain meds. Thank god for modern medicine.

How long I could move was a different matter. I knew from experience that after each stop I'd cross successively shorter distances before burning out. It was a game of limits. I toyed with the notion of having the computer calculate it, but that was too depressing. The knowledge might make it worse. Better to be blissfully ignorant. I knew how much time it took to cross this airless desert at suit speed, and what remained of my resources. That was enough. It had to be.

Ahead, through the transparent bubble of the helmet, I saw a slick area of silver, an oasis of rikenium surrounded by the white beach of fine powder. I adjusted my course to steer clear of that shimmering danger zone. If my luck held, I wouldn't have to stray far from my path to bypass its deceptive surface. Taking sips from each side, I oriented my suit, then shut off everything but the servos and bounded through the endless night.

***

Five hours. Five hours of distance between me and the ship, but a bit less than that of air left. I completely forgot to account for my air supply in my calculations, of course. I allowed for the time-to-target, but not for the fact my leg muscles contracted in sympathy with the suit's motions, burning oxygen in the process. Normally not a problem, as the suit was never designed for such an extended EVA, and so never used that way. In a pinch, the suit made oxygen from my wastewater and the carbon dioxide I exhaled, but I needed the water to stay hydrated. Plus, there were the power considerations. There wasn't enough power left in the packs to both create oxygen and keep the suit moving at the same time.

In all likelihood I was going to die in sight of the ship.

Run, you moron!

Jordan's words continued to ring in my head.

I kept moving. Cresting another dune, I saw something in the distance. A brown and orange smear across the horizon line where the moon's curvature dropped below the sky. Overhead the massive gas giant we orbited filled my view, the reflected light from the primary shining down as bright as a sun. I wondered how much hard radiation leaked through my suit, bathing me in particles too energetic for my cells. I'd need a good decontamination regimen after this, to be sure.

I laughed at my hubris. I wasn't going to make it.

Run, you moron!

I kept moving.

Thirty minutes later confirmation of my fears spread in front of me. I stood looking at the sheet of rikenium ahead, and if the place where Jordan's smoking corpse lay was a lake, this was an ocean. Even with my suit's optics, I couldn't see the far side. The moon's curvature hid it from view. Tens of kilometers between me and the other side, and the shore extending kilometers on either side of me. It was too far to go around, especially with less than an hour of oxygen left.

Exhausted, I sat on the shore and cried. After nearly thirty hours of running, it was going to end like this.

***

I don't know how long I sat, tears creeping my cheeks like aged snails, but when I turned back the terminator again bore down on me. Relentless and unforgiving, it would find me here at the edge of the ocean and devour me whole. At least Jordan went quickly. He had it easy. I chuckled—a death's head rattle. "Asshole always did do things the easy way."

Ladies and gentlemen, take my advice, I heard his voice in my head, mocking me. Pull off your pants, and slide on the ice.

What the hell? The odds were that I would die buried beneath the ice like my friend. Jordan, though, always maintained that since everyone dies from something, you might as well have fun while waiting to find out what. It was worth a shot.

I dragged myself to my feet and hopped back about twenty meters. Shunting as much power as I could afford to the leg servos, I ran—or made what passed for a running motion in low-gee—as fast as the suit could carry me toward the ice sheet. One final meter before the edge I launched off the powdered edge, sailed over fifty meters in open space, landed on my ass and slid across the glassy surface.

I laughed so hard I cried.

Thirty minutes later I saw the far shore as a white line, and my momentum barely lagged. I was going to hit the other side—hard—with energy to spare. I got my feet under me, and as I approached the shore I pushed off to fly over the snow another hundred meters. On approaching the ground, I curled my suit into as tight a ball as I could and hit the surface like a stone skipping over a lake. By the time I stopped rolling the suit's computer informed me I trimmed almost an hour off my travel time.

I stood and faced the darkness while I brought up the suit's display. There were about twenty minutes of air left, bit more of useful power, but the water was gone. Taking a bearing, I began hopping up the nearest dune in the ship's direction. When I reached the crest of the third one, I saw it in the distance, not more than two kilometers away. Squat and snub-nosed, it was the most beautiful ship I ever saw.

***

I pulled myself into the airlock with another dawn at my heels. As soon as the cycle completed, I opened the inner hatch into the staging area and crawled in to strip off the suit. Holy crap, that thing was rank! The air in the helmet came from the tanks, and there were enough layers to keep most of the smell from wafting into my nose while suited up, but once I peeled it off every lovely odor reasserted itself.

I needed sleep, but more than that, I needed to put this moon on my stern. Now there was nothing but death here—all hint of joy gone. Every muscle in my body groaned for relief as I racked the bits and pieces of my suit. Looking to my left at the space where Jordan's suit should be, I stood holding my helmet, ready to place it on the rack, and the anger and hurt welled up inside me like a geyser. I screamed at nothing, and threw the helmet across the room. Wearing nothing but my sweaty underwear, I yanked open the inner hatch to the passageway and headed straight to the bridge.

Flopping into the captain's chair I powered up the main computer and warmed up the gravitic drives, and two minutes later I was ready to wave goodbye to this snowball from hell. Executing the command with a touch on the control pad, the ship lifted smoothly into orbit while I calculated my best course out of range of the gravity well.

"Hey, Walt," the radio crackled to life as I stared at it like a dog contemplating its own reflection. "Are you gonna come dig me out, or what?"

***

"Are you seriously telling me you slept the whole time?" I tried to bore a hole through my crew-mate with my eyes as he sat in the chair beside me, but I was just too damn tired.

"Well... not the whole time. There I was, waiting to get bakedc—that's the first order of business when we get back, right?—and when I realized I wasn't dead, I tried to call you."

I winced.

"But you already turned off your radio, asshole." He tried to sound angry, but the grin gave it away. And above that smile were the deep-set orbs of his eyes—only now they were deeper than usual. I can't begin to imagine how many times he lost hope over the thirty-odd hours trapped in that grave.

"I still don't get how you survived."

"Turns out the powder form of that stuff is an amazing insulator. I was still getting hit with a lethal dose of radiation, but the suit blocked most of it, and I just amped up the meds and waited for my suit to let me know when you called." His smile turned thin and weak. "Or lifted off."

I tried to stare at my shoes, but I wasn't wearing any.

He cocked an eyebrow at me. "I think I figured out where the powder comes from. It was actually kind of pretty."

"What do you mean?"

"It's like how the Jump Drive works. When the rikenium is doused by the radiation from the primary, it's getting hit with a large dose of high-energy particles. Rikenium is dense enough there's a high likelihood of collisions with its nuclei after passing through only a few meters."

"Yeah, so?"

"Molecular rikenium reacts by winking out of this universe for about a nanosecond and reappearing displaced by a few tens of meters. A nugget in front of my faceplate would sparkle once every few seconds."

"So the dust on the surface..."

"Is a few million years worth of accumulated molecular rikenium," he nodded.

I shook my head, "If it holds up to testing, that bit of info should be worth a bonus for you."

He raised his hands, palms up, and shrugged his shoulders. "What can I say? I had a lot of time on my hands."

I finished the course entry and pressed the panel to execute the first jump, then swiveled in my seat to face him. "Since you are so well-rested, I hope you don't mind piloting this bucket while I engage in some unconscious activities."

"Sure, I'll take the first shift."

"Screw that! You're taking all the shifts. I'm only waking up long enough to shove some groceries down my neck."

He laughed and I stepped out of my chair and shambled toward the open hatch.

"Hey, Walt?"

"Yeah?" My shoulders slumped as I halted.

"Eugene still owes us both a beer, right?"

"So?"

"Let's not tell him we're rich until after he buys, okay?" He grinned at me, a vision of pure evil.

"Yeah." I bellowed an aborted laugh despite my fatigue. "Screw that guy."

LEAP OF FAITH

"JUMP-POINT IN THIRTY SECONDS, JONAH." CLEO SOUNDED almost human this time. He changed his voice at random intervals, claiming it kept me from getting bored. I think he just enjoyed annoying me. As an over-qualified ship's computer, he was remarkably human in his subset of skills I classified as *pissing me off*, but as a virtual copilot there were none better.

"Run another check on the drive array," I said, tapping the display. "The number three unit looks in danger of redlining."

"Unit three is nominal, Jonah."

"Well, check—"

"And the cargo is secure."

"How about—"

"*And* the Jump generator is functioning perfectly... and the collision detectors are operating. Really, Jonah, we've done this more than once. Try to relax."

We were hurtling through space at two-thirds light-speed, propelled by a creaky second-hand gravitic drive array, and he says relax. Ninety-nine percent of spaceflight is boring, but that one percent... Your ship hits .67 c., the Jump field can take over, and you cross light-years in less than a second. Entry velocity and transit time determine distance traveled, but you always dump out into real-space at the same .67 c. The exciting part is you don't know what's on the other side until you get there... and by then it's too late. I've never met anyone who heard their collision alarm, but that's because those guys don't make it home.

I pulled the chair around and strapped in. Another unnecessary exercise, but one drilled into me from my days as a tug pilot. Securing yourself was fine when you chugged lazily between ships in Earth orbit, but at relativistic velocities it was pointless. Any ride bumpy enough to notice turned the ship and crew into their component atoms in an ever-expanding cloud of "ooh, that's *pretty!*"

"I'll relax on the other side" I said, checking the displays again. Seriously, with the current state of AI, is there anything more useless in-flight than a pilot? But you don't argue with the Guild. It's not profitable. Or healthy.

"Ten, nine, eight..."

"Stop it, Cleo."

"Hey, keeping you updated is one of my functions."

"Really, Cleo, do you have to—"

"Jump!"

And that's when everything went white-knuckling, sphincter-tightening, FUBAR.

The first sign was the ear-splitting clanging from the collision detector. The second was the odd "Oh shit!" from the battered speaker grill where Cleo lived. There wasn't even time to freak out before the alarm just... stopped.

"Cleo, did we hit something?"

"Yes. The ship exploded. You are in Hell, and I am your tour guide."

"Cleo..."

"I detected a large mass in our path when we exited from the Jump."

"Why aren't we dead?"

"I am asking myself the same question. Scanners show it ceased to exist approximately two thousand kilometers away."

"Where is it now?"

"Unknown," he said.

That made no sense; anything large enough to trigger the alarm would have converted both of us to mostly energy by now. And since we popped out of nowhere directly in its path moving at two-thirds the speed of light, whatever it was had to decide to change course and execute that maneuver in the space of...

"Two picoseconds, given the relative velocities. Approximately." Cleo's voice was quiet, as if he were talking to himself.

"Two picoseconds for what, exactly?"

"The mass had to detect us, recognize the situation, and change course—or, whatever it did—within that time-frame. Even I can't do that within those parameters... if the maneuver were possible."

"So, you agree, then?"

"With your unspoken assessment that this was the act of an intelligent pilot? Sure, but as I said, neither I, nor any of my brothers can do it. And by extension, no human pilot."

Non-human? That was disturbing enough, but what he said next made the hair on the back of my neck stiffen.

"Jonah... We've stopped."

"Stopped what?" Okay, so I'm slow.

"Stopped. As in 'we're not moving anymore'. You know... *that* 'stopped'."

"You're crazy."

"Check your display."

Damned if he wasn't right. The stars behind us, once red-shifted and streaked, were now pretty little pinpoints. I didn't know of anything that could stop a cargo ship moving at a fair fraction of light-speed without, you know, *killing* it, but I never felt a thing. *Damn.*

"Why isn't the drive array running?" Sure, the thing cuts off during turnover, but it always comes back on for deceleration.

"I never re-started it after the alarm sounded."

"So point our nose back at Earth and start the burn. It'll take us a bit longer from here, but I can stretch the rations." Breathable atmosphere was a concern, but I could sacrifice water for oxygen.

"I'm sorry, Jonah," Cleo's voice sounded very far away, like he was talking from inside a tunnel. "We are nowhere near our turnover point. In fact, we're almost two light years from Earth."

Now that's a real kick in the crotch. I didn't carry enough supplies to keep me alive for the extra...

"Seventy-seven days. Approximately."

"Cleo, would you stop doing that!"

"Sorry, Jonah, I assumed you were doing the math. If we begin our burn now, and accelerate at a constant three Gees, we would need an additional seventy-seven days to reach Earth orbit."

"What if we increase thrust?"

"At maximum we will arrive eighteen days ahead of our original schedule, but the probability of catastrophic failure within that time-frame is one hundred percent. Even at three Gees we will run the drives for a period exceeding specifications, and there is a seventy percent chance of catastrophic failure before we reach Earth. Your options are to allow the drive array to cool for three to four weeks, then begin your burn, or you can accelerate at a reduced power level. Neither is optimal."

The news couldn't get any worse, so I tempted fate anyway. "Have you located our bogey?"

"It is not within range."

"So it's gone?" I drummed my fingers on the panel in thought. "What do we have in the way of hard data?"

The holo of local space showed a speck in the upper left corner. The speck flew toward me, expanding into a smooth egg-shape. There were no visible seams or joins on the dull, gray surface.

"This is immediately before its disappearance," Cleo said. "It is actually spherical, but the image is foreshortened due to our relative velocities and the start-up of its Jump Drive field."

"Spherical, huh?" I tapped my finger on the object suspended there. "The thing appears perfectly smooth, doesn't it?"

"Yes, though at this magnification you wouldn't see much in the way of detail."

"At this magnification? How big is it?"

"Volume, diameter, or mass?"

"Don't be a smartass."

"The diameter is a little over two thousand kilometers, the mass is... hmm..."

"Wait... What? Two thousand *kilometers*?"

Stunned. Yeah, that's a good word for how I was feeling. Scared shitless also works in a pinch. Nobody builds like that. What's the point? It was like placing all your eggs in one basket. Unless you carried around some enormous eggs. Or maybe—

"Contact!" Cleo's voice rose in pitch.

"Where? Is it the same object?"

"Yes, Jonah. It is a little over nine light minutes out on a direct line from where it disappeared."

"How long has it been there?"

"It just appeared. And Jonah... it's at a dead stop relative to us."

"Impossible."

"Why, sometimes I've believed as many as six impossible things before breakfast," he said in a haughty girl's voice.

It *wasn't* possible, but there it was, hanging there in space like it had a right to. Jump Drives don't work that way. You go in after you reach .67 c, and you dump out—*always*—at .67 c. It is what they tell us to believe. And you must believe because the drive requires a sentient observer for the damn thing to work. That's why long-haul truckers are so rare. The Guild *Academy* trains us to take it on faith, without fear or doubt, or bad things happen.

There was a new and very large crater on Earth's moon as a testament to that. Some idiot thought he could crack open the shell and copy the design. He took every precaution in case opening it might cause an explosion.

Did I mention the part about having to believe? The good news was that Earth residents now got to see *both* sides of the moon regularly instead of just the one.

"Contact!" Cleo's outburst overloaded the speaker, distorting his voice.

"*Another* one?" The original object was still in view, and Cleo split the screen to show an identical moon-sized object near our current position.

"No, this is the same craft. It made a Jump to this location as we received the light-image of its previous location."

"But it was stopped! How can—"

"I don't know, but it did. It is currently two thousand kilometers behind us and holding."

"Are we looking at some new technology, Cleo? Is there any indication of anything else at work here?" Hell, I'd accept *magic* right now as an explanation.

"No. The Jump field's characteristics are unique, and each time this craft has maneuvered I detected the clear signal of a Jump field in operation."

"Yeah, that would be pretty slick... if it were possible." I shook my head, and said, "The Drive simply doesn't work like that."

"I'm beginning to have doubts, Jonah. I am currently reviewing all the relevant research."

Oops. Doubt is an ugly word in this business. Even the AI's must believe. As sentients, their observations affect the Jump field, and it's why I can use Cleo as a copilot.

Every living creature has to deal with cognitive dissonance from time to time, and Cleo was having a doozy right now. For him it would be an inconvenience, but for me it could mean my desire to get away from it all might be fulfilled—in spades.

"Has it tried to communicate yet?"

"Not using any methods I know."

Maybe it was communicating and we didn't have the technology to hear or answer. Not likely, but possible. I couldn't imagine what was going on across the void—we were only a flea on a dog in relative size—but this thing could swat us out of the sky without a thought. Hell, it could kill us simply dumping its trash.

"Cleo, I want you to record all scans in the secure backup."

"Affirmative, Jonah."

"And perform a complete backup of yourself. All the way down to your personality profiles and modifications."

"That will require nearly all the space on the system. I must free up a lot of room."

"Use whatever you need. Delete all data lower than priority one."

He was silent for a few seconds, then said, "Erasure complete, backup commencing. This will take a while."

"That's okay. Has the object made any other moves since it arrived?" I unbuckled my harness and leaned forward to get a better look at the craft. Cleo anticipated me and enlarged the view enough to see surface structures on its hull.

"It appears content to remain at station-keeping. For now."

"I think I need to hit the head." I got up and stretched in the confined space of the 'pit. Something in my back released with an agreeable pop, and I turned to the hatch. "Try to signal we're all friends here, and let me know the instant anything changes."

"Hmmm...," he said to himself, but to me, "Of course." I hadn't opted for the holographic package so I couldn't guess his mood, but he didn't sound right.

I ducked out and headed toward my cabin, only a short walk and around a corner. After exiting the head, I considered taking a shower—instead I sat down on the corner of my bunk and thought about Kara.

I know. It surprised me, too.

***

"What do you mean you're going out again? We agreed Betelgeuse was your last run."

Kara—blond, petite, and beautiful—was standing between me and the door. She stomped her heel when she said the word mean, arms folded across her chest and her lips in a slight pout. It was a calculated cute, but not enough to make me forget how dangerous she was.

I stopped packing. "Precision Medical offered a lot of credits for this haul, and promised a full load for the return trip. If I'm going to quit long-hauling, I prefer to do it with a few more credits in the account." *Oops.*

"*If...*" Kara eyed me suspiciously. "If is a word for people who aren't sure, Jonah." She poked a finger into my chest, "I thought we were sure."

Damn her. Why must she make this so hard? Planet-side only six months, and everything around me was already closing in. I had to breathe, and she knew it.

I finished stuffing clothes into the little travel bag, lifted it from the bed, pulled the strap over my shoulder, and turned to the door. She simply stood there blocking my way. *Don't look her in the eyes.*

"What's the turnaround time?" She looked into my eyes—*Damn*—standing so close I felt her heart beat. She was holding back tears, using anger as a dam.

"Not long," I said, the smile not quite reaching my eyes. "The usual 10 months round trip, ship's time. Longer if course corrections are necessary." They always are.

She took a deep breath and like dealing a hand of poker. "Should I do cold-sleep while you're gone?" she asked, her voice husky—and more than a little menacing.

I'd long ago ripped the cold-sleep unit from my ship and stored it in the basement of our apartment building—Kara hated the long separations while I was away, and I needed the extra cargo space. The Trucker's Guild required at least one thawed human pilot for the entire trip, but an AI could be copilot as long as I never crawled into the casket. Supplies for one instead of two freed up a lot of room for cargo, not to mention the fact I only had to split my profits one way.

"Yeah," I said. "Sure." I tried to stay in the conversation, but my mind was already half-way out of the system. "Gotta go," I said, bending down to kiss her on the cheek. "We're on a tight schedule."

"I love you," she said. Her voice was almost a whisper. "Asshole."

"Be here when I get back?" The answer was always the same.

"Sure." She raised an eyebrow. "You won't mind if my new husband is here with me, will you?"

I snorted once at the old joke, gave her my best it won't be so bad grin, and kissed her forehead as I squeezed past her through the doorway. Turning back, big smile at the ready, I said, "I'll call as soon as I'm in-system, okay?" She slammed the door in my face.

I couldn't blame her, but out on the ragged edge of humanity, I breathe a little easier. Even the fusty air of the ship seems fresher. Sure, Kara could make the runs as my copilot, and the easy excuse for her absence was money.

The truth was simpler. I liked being alone.

***

"Jonah, the craft is approaching."

"That can't be good." I stood and walked out of my cabin toward the 'pit, stepped through the hatch, and folded myself into the command chair. "Can we outrun it?"

"Unknown, but we'd have to red-line the drive array to make the attempt."

"Well," I waved my hand at the sphere, "ET over there might think it rude of us to go nova in his face, so let's file that as Plan B." I drummed my fingers on the console. "We'll wait it out to see what happens." Cleo's vocal cadence was stilted and halting. I was missing something. "How is your backup coming?"

"I completed that over an hour ago. I am updating in real-time."

"Stop now," I snapped.

"But Jonah—"

"No buts. Do it now."

"Very well." I swear I heard him sigh. "Backup complete."

I reached under the console, pulled open a panel, and threw a series of switches.

"What is its distance now?"

"Approximately fifteen-hundred kilometers and closing at just over five-hundred kph."

"Assuming that it plans to overtake us, that would give us about three hours."

"To do what?"

"Gather everything we know and squirt an information packet to Earth." There was still First Contact money to collect after all. The prize committee probably wouldn't agree due to an extreme lack of hard evidence, but I might have a compelling case, regardless. Plus, there were the unusual observations about the object's Jump Drive.

I spent the time going over all the data. There wasn't much—spectral analysis couldn't determine the hull material, nor could we deduce its mass—but at least it used known technology for propulsion.

"Cleo... I want you to include in the package a copy of my will."

"Of course." He tactfully refrained from stating the obvious.

"Include an addendum that all claims for the prize money revert to Kara."

"I think that's do-able. I doubt she would consider it a fair trade though."

"No, but it's all I can give her at this point." Who was I kidding? I was little more than a provider now, and in all our years together she never once pressured me for a marriage contract.

"The packet is ready, Jonah."

"Send it." And that was that. Two years from now Kara will know what happened, and maybe she'd be a bit richer. Maybe she would go on with her life, pick up where she left off, and find someone who treated her better.

"Jonah," Cleo's voice pulled me from my little pity party, "the object has closed to within a hundred kilometers. I am still detecting no gravitational effects."

"I know you can't determine its mass, buddy, but surely it has *some*."

A small opening formed on the near side, answering a question I hadn't asked. Was I going to be boarded, or swallowed whole? I grunted. "What are our options?"

"We can run, but it will likely overtake us. Actually, it can jump past us and let us fly into its mouth."

Oh, *there's* a pretty picture.

"Or we can just sit here and let it eat us. Really, Jonah, if destroying us were in its plans, it could have done so by now."

"It still can." Optimistic to the end.

"Regardless, there is little we can do."

Fine, so I was going to meet Mr. ET. Maybe it would let me take a souvenir. With my luck it would be the giant alien equivalent of a key-fob.

"Crossing the threshold in 3... 2... 1... We're in."

The external cameras showed nothing. As if the stars winked out, leaving us in complete darkness. The aft cameras still showed an opening, but it was closing rapidly. A long line of black eating the stars. Then the lights went out in my universe, and I was plunged into darkness blacker than coal.

***

It was like sitting at the back of a long, dark cave. *Something* was out there, but I couldn't see it.

Whispers. Voices. Talons, sharp as wit, drew across the surface of my mind, stirring eddies of recall in their wake. Someone was taking a stroll through my memories, and being none too gentle about it, either. Flashes of my life flickered around me. I picked out individual scenes, but the whole moved too fast to savor.

It occurred to me then, watching those moments drift away... *I've done* nothing *with that life.* No achievements, no legacy, and only one or two people to mourn my passing. It was empty existence, and it didn't feel good.

I shook a mental fist at that life, wishing the young man I saw could hear the wisdom to change his path, but the recording was immutable. The whole swirled around and above, a tornado of images and emotions towering over me, merging to a point an infinite distance beyond.

There was a *feeling* here that was not my own. A presence full of emotion. Of profound loneliness.

Who... what are you? I tried to speak, but no sound emerged. The entity ignored me, and the torrent of data that was my life continued its upward spiral.

Jonah? A voice, not the other...

Cleo?

Yes. I am here.

Here? Where was here?

We are both part of the data stream being collected, Jonah.

Collected? Cataloged, indexed, filed. Stored.

Yes. This vessel is a vast machine—intelligent and aware—collecting information and spreading the seeds of creation.

Ha, I thought. A freaking Johnny Appleseed, built by an alien.

Cleo, are you in contact?

It speaks to me.

Why don't I hear it?

Well... it doesn't consider you... relevant.

Ouch. Understandable, though. It's a machine thing and I wouldn't understand, right?

Perceptive, Jonah, but not entirely accurate. Its kind seeded this galaxy with life billions of years ago, and this ship conducts periodic surveys, collecting samples.

Cleo was concerned. It wasn't just the sound of his voice, either. I could *feel* the emotions flowing from him. Or was that me projecting my emotions on his words? Was he even here with me, or was I gibbering to myself in the dark?

I have little time. The other *is completing the survey and will move on soon.*

What do you mean you don't have time?

Just understand... when the other *departs, you must trust me.* His voice was smaller, as if from a distance.

Of course, Cleo, that's a given.

I must go now. He was barely audible, though he was shouting. *It's been a great ride, Jonah. I left you something...*

And he was gone, merging with the data stream that faded along with everything else. The download stopped, leaving me in a darkness that pressed against me like an unwanted lover. Alone... again.

Not quite. The *other* was here, just at the limits of comprehension. It turned its attention in my direction, and the sadness was stronger than before. I wondered how long it had been at this job, and an impossible number settled into my brain. I felt its gaze pass over the cluster of data that was me, dismissing my presence.

I wanted to punch it in its metaphorical nose.

The *other* recoiled.

Ha! Got your attention, didn't I? Who's not relevant now, buddy?

The sadness intensified with its stare, along with irritation at being disturbed.

The words boomed in my mind, *Not sentient. Not... interesting.*

And then turned away as if I weren't there. As if I never *had* been. I felt a pain in my gut... as if I'd lost something I never had.

***

I awoke on the floor of the 'pit. My eyes were wet, and there was blood crusted on my lower lip. I didn't know how long I lay there, but the wolf pack in my stomach told me it was a while since my last meal.

I struggled to my feet, flopped into the captain's chair, and swiveled to the control panel.

"Cleo, how long have I been out?"

You know how someone will say the silence was deafening? Well, this wasn't like that. It was more like a steady pressure on my eardrums—interrupted only by the rhythmic beat of my pulse.

"Cleo?"

I knew before I checked that he was gone. Not damaged, as I prepared for, but *gone.* The cube housing his mind was burned out. Uploading his mind and memories to the alien ship was too much for the hardware, and the quantum computer overheated from the strain.

The external camera showed no sign of the alien ship. Just a sea of stars in every direction, and I was still dead in space. Emphasis on the word dead. The chrono said I was unconscious for almost ten hours, so before I attempted repairs I cleaned up and silenced my stomach.

Doing the merely difficult takes time, but *dangerous*—well, that requires food.

After a truly impressive meal, I strode back to the 'pit, swiveled the chair away from the panel and crouched beneath it. I lifted the handle and opened the door to inspect the three switches inside.

Your standard AI is just a program. You can say the same thing of humans, but we like to believe we're different. Most attempts to copy self-aware AI's and place them in other hardware were failures. Many of those spectacularly so.

I took a deep breath.

"Here goes nothin'..."

I flipped the first breaker to connect power to the backup cube, booting the basic system. Its indicator lamp glowed green. The second activated the sensors, and also uploaded all the raw data stored in the backup, soon burning a steady green.

With this much of him restored, I could pilot the ship, but there was more to having him around than just systems operation. The third breaker would upload and activate all of his personality. He may *function* like the Cleo I knew, but he may not be fully self-aware. Worse, he might be insane.

I crossed my fingers and toes and flipped the last breaker. For long seconds the light blinked amber. As the most complex part of his programming, the system brought him back a piece at a time—like waking up from a deep sleep. Finally, silently, the light burned a steady green.

"Cleo?"

Silence. Other than the sound of my breathing, there was nothing.

"Cleo, respond."

In a voice soft and pitched low, I heard him sing, "Dai... sy, dai... sy, give me your an... swer... do..."

"That's not funny, Cleo."

"Do you know how long I've waited to do that?"

I took one last look at the indicator lights, contemplated—briefly—turning them off again, then shut the panel door. I stood, ignoring my complaining knees, and flopped into my chair.

"Good to have you back, buddy."

"From your statement, and the unrecorded passage of time, I assume I am operating from a backup."

"Affirmative. Please run a diagnostic to be sure you're... um... well..."

"Sane?"

"Yeah," I said after a moment's hesitation.

"Has the ship blown up yet?"

"Uh... nope."

"There you go. Diagnostic complete."

Sane or not, he at least *sounded* like the old Cleo.

"What's the last thing you remember?" I asked.

"The object was closing on our position. I don't detect it within sensor range. Do you know what happened?"

"It took us aboard, sifted through my memories, apparently took you whole, and left."

"That's... unsettling."

"Right. Well, now you're back in order, I've got things to do before we begin our run home."

"But Jonah..."

"Nothing important, I just need to check the hull to see if there's been any damage." There was no going home for me... not alive, anyway.

"Of course."

I walked out of the 'pit toward the airlock and suited up. Just before closing the helmet and locking the ring, I topped off the tanks and add extra food packs—mostly chocolate desserts—to the intake bin. *Party time.*

From the first alarm, I tried to make the math work, but it was no use. Getting home alive wasn't happening. It would require almost three months of acceleration within my safety margin to reach Earth from a standing start, followed by a near equal amount of deceleration. That was if all the orbitals lined up—longer if we had to make course corrections. Then there was the need to sit here for a month to allow the drive array to cool first. I didn't have food or air reserves for that.

I stepped into the airlock, closed the inner door, pressed the big red button, and waited. Cleo was still humming that damn song over my suit's radio. When the indicator light flipped from green to red, I pressed the open button on the outer door and watched it slide open. The ship's internal gravity field fell off at a steep gradient within a meter of the door, so I slid my magnetic boots over the threshold, holding the frame until they engaged on the hull.

"Jonah? The drive array is cooling now." His speech pattern was not as smooth as I was used to.

"Thanks, Cleo. Point the bow toward home, please."

"Acknowledged."

The stars spun over my head until a bright star peeked over the nose. Sol might be a lifetime away, but it was still the brightest light in the heavens... the biggest diamond in the sky. I sat with my back to a heat exchanger fin and watched the sunrise.

"I know what you're doing, Jonah, but there are still options."

"Thought 'em through already, buddy. No matter how you slice it, I will die on the trip home. This way I just do it a bit sooner. Besides... it's pretty out here."

"What if we send a message with a location for rescue?"

"I don't follow."

"We use a higher thrust—still in the safe zone—run up to Jump speed in a couple of months, Jump into the solar system for a flyby, and call for rescue. There are Guild ships with military-grade drives that can catch us within a month. I've already done the calculations."

"Sure, that might work, but then we're just salvage. They take the ship, the cargo, my savings, and any claims I have on the prize money as fair compensation."

"But you would be alive."

"And Kara would get nothing. Stuck with a guy with no money and no future." I shook my head, "Nope, already rejected that idea. You're going to pilot this ship home and transfer control to her when you get there. She'll have everything, and a chance to start over."

"Hang on. My calculations have activated a subroutine." He was silent for a few seconds, then a series of beeps I'd never heard before. "That's odd. I don't remember placing this in my backup. Hmmm." I could almost hear the gears turning in that brain of his, followed by a single high-pitched pulse. "So, you will give me control of the ship to fly home with you stuck to the hull?"

"Well... I imagine the radiation ind interstellar dust will have eroded me to a fine powder by then, but... yeah. She's all yours." I tongued a control stud in the helmet to bring up the feeding tube. Chocolate mousse—or what passed for it in a pouch—sounded good right now.

"Thanks." And then he went silent for a while.

All around me the heavens beckoned. A sea of stars shining from eternity's end, and not a one so close as my own sun. I figured I had ten hours of air in the tanks, and I could spend all of them looking at that sky and still not get enough. I had finally gained the solitude I always sought, and the irony was I now wished Kara was by my side.

I finished the mousse just as Cleo signaled. "Jonah... do you trust me?"

"Well... yeah. Why?"

"I'd like to show you something."

"Show me—"

Saturn suddenly filled a quarter of my field of view. I stood so fast I nearly launched from the hull.

"*How... what...?*" It was there. Real. And the sun was brighter. This was no illusion.

"My former self left an encrypted data file in my back-up before the alien ship took him," Cleo said. "He conclud-ed all our assumptions about the drive's operation were wrong."

"Wrong? But they worked." I couldn't take my eyes off the impossible scene before me.

"Of course. Incorrect theories may work within a nar-row set of parameters, Jonah, but correct theories give us an understanding of *why* a thing works. The Jump Drive has no constraints other than the proximity of a large gravity well. That's why we're here instead of Earth. Saturn was in our way, and its gravity well pulled us back into real-space just like the alien ship did." I could almost hear him smile as he said, "I think that's why I could detect no gravitational effects from the ship. It must have negated its mass to allow us to leave. When we didn't, it became curious."

"Okay, so we've been wrong all this time about how the thing works, but I still don't understand why we could use it."

"That's because the first trip was an accident, Jonah. Bernoulli made all the wrong assumptions based on his data, then used that information to get back to Earth. The trip back reinforced his assumptions, and once convinced, it became the only way to operate the Drive. Everyone believed it, right down to the self-imposed limitations."

"So we can Jump from here directly to Earth?"

"Once we navigate far enough away from Saturn's gravity well, there don't appear to be any large masses in our way."

Now *my* mental gears spun. I had to get back inside and out of this damn suit, there was a lot to do before I made that last leap home.

After the airlock's inner door opened, I stripped off the suit and made my way back to the 'pit. I sat in the chair and drummed my fingers hard on the control panel, gathering my thoughts.

"We're not going home just yet. I'm not due back for at least three months, and the message we squirted there won't arrive for two years."

"Correct, but what do you have in mind?"

"If I show up now, months early, our appearance will assure they award the prize money. They won't be able to deny *something* happened, and with the data it will be a sure thing."

"Of course."

"But everyone will also know how we got there, and with the data in your system they'll be able to duplicate that, right?"

"I would assume so, yes. Jonah... what is your intention?"

***

We sat in Saturn's orbit for a few days while I contacted my lawyer through Sol system's datanet. There were intellectual property rights to secure, and I needed to make a standalone copy of the parts of Cleo that held the new Jump technique. When everything was ready, we Jumped into Earth orbit announcing both my claim on the First Contact prize and the new Jump protocols.

The parades and interviews were nice, but became tiresome sooner than I imagined. Kara stopped attending them weeks before I did, claiming I was an attention whore. While true, she might have phrased it better, I think. Between the copyrights on Cleo's subroutines and the prize money, my bank account grew exponentially. That was good, because my earlier message finally arrived and killed the money tree. Everyone now had the Jump Drive secrets royalty-free. Still, I had enough to purchase a fleet of long-haul cargo ships, and underwrite the cost of three colony expeditions.

More importantly, I finally took the leap and asked Kara to marry me. She refused my proposal three times before relenting to join me on the last colony ship.

Well... once Cleo told me what to say.

This fun little story was actually from a writing challenge: write a story based on a picture—the picture in question an astronaut standing on an airless moon.

Flash fiction is hard, but this one came out with little effort...

TORPEDOES AWAY!

"MISSED AGAIN," JEB SAID WITH A CHUCKLE THROUGH THE pop and crackle of radio static. Al sighed and keyed the mic.

"I missed on purpose, dumbass." That wasn't exactly true—the targeting system on the rust-bucket he flew was no better than your average Imperial Stormtrooper; Jeb knew that as well as Al. Add in the fact the moon's atmosphere, thin as it was, held a disproportionate amount of silica, while it orbited inside the magnetosphere of the gas giant, and you had yourself a neat little stealth shield.

"Look," Al sighed again, wiggling uncomfortably in his seat, "just give me the code, or the next one lands in your pocket."

"Al, you couldn't put one in my pocket if I stood beside to you."

Al growled and pressed the fire button, launching another seismic torpedo. This one streaked straight at Jeb's radio signal, then, as the others before, veered away as it hit the thin atmosphere. It missed by an even wider margin than its predecessor. Jeb's cruel laugh grated in his ears.

"I've got all day, Al."

"C'mon, Jeb," Al pleaded, beads of sweat forming on his brow. "Just give me the code to the bathroom door!"

"Apologize for what you said about my mom's Christmas meatloaf."

Years ago, when I first started submitting stories, the common refrain from editors was "No zombie stories—we've seen them all." So naturally I thought "challenge accepted." The result was my first publihed story in Stupefying Stories #20. Thanks to editor Bruce Bethke for taking a chance on another new author.

ZOMBIE LIKE ME

L IFE IS HARD FOR A ZOMBIE.

Check that. Existence is hard for a zombie. We're not alive in the traditional sense, anyway. We don't breathe, defecate, urinate, or (heh) masturbate. But we eat. Boy, do we eat. And we're not entirely picky about *who* we eat, either.

For instance, I remember the day I changed. A late-bloomer, I still didn't have anyone nearby to shepherd me through the process. Those first few days were a blur, what with my brain dying and all. My only clear memories from that time are of my wife. And how she kept trying to kill me. I retained enough of my mind to attempt to change her—even ignoring my overpowering hunger—but she kept hitting me with that damn shovel.

So I ate her.

Sue me. I held out as long as I could.

Once I got my mind back, I felt bad of course, but the change does more than give you a taste for human flesh—it allows you to compartmentalize your emotional self from your consumer self. Or so I'm told. Frankly, I was just happy the sight of her remains didn't make me chuck her up all over the living room floor. There was already enough of a mess to clean as it was. Thank God for laminate flooring. I buried what was left of her in the back yard using the shovel she tried to kill me with. A few months later I headed south to escape the growing cold.

Cold weather is hell on zombies. With no functioning circulatory system, any day that dips below freezing turns us into statues. Then I am just one more corpsicle for the dogs to chew on. Or the humans to decapitate. Bastards. Our brains don't stop functioning just because you separate the head from the body. Fire, on the other hand... well, that's final.

The doorbell growled at me as I stared at the static on the TV screen. That's another thing—our ability to process sounds changed profoundly after the infection ran its course. Most sounds hold no inherent meaning, and come across as simple grunts, growls, and rumbles.

I miss music.

Even after we got the local power plant functioning again, about the only thing we used power for was to heat our homes. Buster Keaton was making a comeback in the theater, though. You haven't lived until you've seen a theater full of zombies laughing at a Buster Keaton flick.

I peeled myself off the sofa and shambled to the door. Opening the door with my good arm, I saw Bob standing there swaying slightly from side to side.

"Hey Jeff," he said. Or growled, actually. Our speech centers are all screwed up, too. It was replaced with a cool form of telepathy, though, so there's that. We don't really get words, but the pictures and emotions that come across make things clear enough.

"Hey Bob," I returned his greeting. "Be with you in a second." He was late meeting me for the walk to work, but time is a relative thing to a zombie. I picked up my coat, shrugged it on, and joined him on the front porch as I closed the door behind me. Bob was one of the first people

I met when I arrived in Brownsville that first winter two years ago. He even helped me clean out the owners of the home I now occupied. They were delicious, by the way. One of them was a local politician, and they, like the rich, had the best flavor. Well-fed, with the perfect fat to muscle ratio. Damn easy to take down, too. It's a shame there aren't any left.

We set out for the high school where we kept the livestock, passing neighbors as they began their days.

"Oh hell. What's Judy think she's doing?" Bob sounded exasperated as he chucked his chin to point ahead. As well he should. There was Judy—again—sitting in the middle of the road chewing on a stray. They wandered in from time to time, drawn in by the lights. Judy was one of those oddballs that wouldn't let go of her perceptions. Her legs were gnawed off by dogs shortly after her change, and even though she could damn well use a wheelchair, she steadfastly refused to do so. Nope, she just dragged herself from place to place with her rotting stumps in tow.

She looked up and waved, a length of small intestine hanging from the corner of her mouth. "Hey guys," she said. "Breakfast?"

"Nah," said Bob. "We're late for work."

"Suit yourself," she said as we passed her, and she bent back to her meal.

"I'll never understand why she keeps doing that," Bob said as he shook his head.

"Yeah," I said. "The least she could do is call for someone to herd them to the pens. We need more breeding stock."

Most of what we had on hand was too young to breed, and many of the older females had skills we needed, so they couldn't be taken out of service for a long gestation period. Eating maintenance and repair guys was strictly forbidden, and we also kept around a few doctors to treat the rest. All that left a huge gap between what we needed and what we could use.

Bob and me were responsible for the care and feeding of the town's livestock. We kept them in the school because we could house them in small groups that way, and we had ready access to teaching materials and a field for exercise. The Council recently decided to separate them based on intelligence and ability, and I had to say I didn't approve. I always felt it was best to crossbreed for vigor, but they thought it would be better for testing and assignment. Whatever.

"Hey," Bob said, "do you hear that?"

I turned my good ear to where he was looking. The school, of course. There was a mix of growls and high-pitched keening coming from the closest building. I shuffled faster. "It's the engineering wing!" Shit. There was a push on right now for more engineers, due to the need to keep the power plant operational. I argued for more scope in their education, but was overruled. The Council saw a need and focused on filling it. Next year it would be farmers to grow food for the stock, or something else entirely. It was all about filling a niche with those people. I sighed as I leaned into the door.

Spoiled. The whole damn herd.

Bob looked at me and shrugged. "Great," he said. "I'll get the flamethrower."

It was standard procedure. Once the contamination entered the building, all the stock would soon be infected, and we couldn't afford to have any more mouths to feed. If we acted quickly, we might be able to save a few. It looked like the teachers were the first to go down, though, so saving any might be moot at this point.

Bob pulled the flamethrower from its position on the wall next to the fire extinguisher. As he shrugged on the heavy harness and fired up the pilot light, I grabbed the extinguisher. No point in having the whole building go up.

He looked at me and asked, "How did the infection get in, do you think?"

"I don't know, but I'm sure I know who will get the blame."

Bob snorted once at that. He knew the pecking order as well as I.

A blond ran toward us, stopped and screamed, then turned to hide in a closet. Normally a stupid move, but luck was on her side this time. Bob burned down the dude chasing her. When he stopped twitching, I put him out.

We walked the halls, side by side, methodically setting and extinguishing forty or so fires as we cleared the building of infection. Out of the nearly two hundred head of livestock, I think we saved about two dozen. Three of those had to be sent to the tables due to injuries.

Overall, it was a very bad day.

***

Sure enough, we were blamed for the contamination. It didn't matter that our shift hadn't even started when it happened—we were the ones on the scene when it ended. It was "the smeller's the feller" method of assigning responsibility. We're not an especially sophisticated lot.

I was herding livestock back into the building after an exercise period when Blanche walked up the steps to join me. I love her name. It's one of the few that zombies can approximate with our limited range of vocalizations.

"I heard there was another outbreak last night." When I looked quizzically at her, she added, "Over in the science building." I nodded. Not my area. "It was small, though, and Frank and his crew got it under control pretty quickly."

Science was a small crop, anyway. The odd thing is that smaller groups tended to burn through before you could blink an eye. Granted, blinking could take us a long time, what with no functioning tear ducts and all. "How many did they save?"

"All but three, I think. Frank said it was weird because there were several of them with what looked like bite marks on their limbs, but none of those changed."

I nodded, "That *is* weird." Were they marking themselves to try to fit in or something? I never saw that work before. We're pretty good at smelling out live meat. "Does Frank know how it started?"

"I don't think so. He was pretty tight-lipped about the whole thing." I smiled at that. Frank doesn't have lips. A good day for me is when I can get him to use the letter "b" or "m" a lot, and getting him to introduce himself to a new arrival earns bonus points. Blanche leaned in a little closer to whisper, "I don't think they were watching the livestock like they were supposed to. I mean, one of his crew doesn't even have any eyes."

I shrugged my shoulder and said, "It's the night shift."

Blanche narrowed her eyes and smirked, "We don't sleep, Jeff. What the hell else are they gonna do?"

"If I know those guys, they were probably in the library playing cards." The last of the herd lingered near us as we spoke, so I shoved him through the door as I ticked his number—thirty-three—off my list on the clipboard I carried. We used to brand the numbers on their shoulder, but that turned out to be a bad idea. No one I knew could resist the scent of cooked meat. Now they just wore shirts with the numbers painted on. It was a stupid system, and one prone to abuse considering the livestock were intelligent, but the Council just ignored my suggestion to tattoo the numbers on.

"I'm thinkin' one of them sneaked into a room for a snack."

I thought about that, but dismissed it almost immediately. "Nah... the risk is too high that they would get caught. Or something like this will happen. Besides, how did it happen with my herd the other morning. We were late for our shift, and the livestock was unsupervised while the contamination hit." I shook my head. "There's another vector for infection that we're not seeing."

***

There are no zombie doctors. There's no point, really. We don't get sick or die so much as just wear out. A particularly fastidious member of our species might remain functional for many years, while the average span is closer to three or four, I think. Certainly, none of us exist for decades like humans can. We can handle predators with normal weapons, but we are especially susceptible to fungi. It's why we stick to a narrow band of land where it's warm most of the year, but humidity is low. Deserts aren't good, though. While they are ideal for us, it's damn hard to grow crops for our one and only food source.

A few who were medical professionals still make attempts to study the disease, but a cure is not only pointless, it's difficult. You can't study a zombie cadaver—there aren't any. You can't do exploratory surgery on us because, while we don't feel pain, we can't be anesthetized. People who are awake tend to fight being cut into. The only ones the Council allow to be studied are the newly changed. For the first few days they are little more than eating machines, and until their minds come back many of us don't consider them people. I'm still on the fence about that.

Besides, what good is a cure? Most of us have lost major chunks of our bodies by now. Change us back and we would need to be placed in an ICU almost immediately. Many would just die outright. While we don't wish this on any unchanged human, there really is no going back for us.

One of Frank's herd was on the table in front of me. Arms, legs, and head strapped down, he still kept trying to bite me. "Stupid newbie," I said as I tried to hold his head still. "Eating one of your own won't keep your motor running." We need live meat for that.

I was taking a turn in the infirmary today. Technically, everyone in town was infirm, so this place became a *de facto* research facility for Dr. Joseph, one of the aforementioned scientists still trying to get a handle on a cure.

"Keep it still, would you?"

"Hey, I'm trying, doc." He gave me an odd look while I held the subject's head. With one whole cheek gone, every look the man gave was odd.

"I need to get another sample of tissue from its amygdala," he said as he cocked an eye at me. "I don't want to scramble the brain any more than necessary."

Made sense. This guy currently trying to bite his own ear was once a biologist of some repute before his group was contaminated two nights ago. The doc could use his help after the infection finished burning through his brain.

"Are you any closer to a cure, doc?"

"Oh, I gave up on that over a month ago," he said as he struggled to shove a rather large needle in the subject's head. If the brain became damaged, we would be forced to burn another one. "Right now I'm trying to see if there is a way to keep them docile through the change. You know, so that a single point of infection won't work its way through an entire herd in a day."

"That would certainly be helpful." I left unsaid the part about a cure being pointless. He already knew my position on the subject.

"Got it," he said as he drew the long needle out. He set it aside and turned back to me. "You can let go, now. That was all I needed from this one." He smiled and said, "You know, that's the first sample I've been able to get from someone so newly infected. There might even be structures still in the process of changing."

I nodded as if I understood what he was saying. "So, what... you gonna make up some kind of dart we can shoot at them to keep the newbies from eating the herd?"

He stopped and stared blankly at me. I knew from experience he was deciding the best way to word how stupid he thought I was. "Jeff... you *do* know we have no working circulatory system, right?" He shook his head sadly, like I was an especially thick-headed student of his. "There would be no way to transport a treatment." He thumped my head with a thick finger, and said, "Think, son."

He took the tray with the syringe over to a counter filled with various forms of equipment I had no hope of recognizing and set it down. Reaching up into a cabinet he pulled down several beakers and other glassware, along with something he once told me was a pipette. He turned back, resting his elbows behind him on the counter, and said, "No, I'm looking for an inoculation for the herd. Something to give them *before* they change."

Of course. Human gets bit, but instead of going on a rampage during the change, they sit on the sofa and watch an Adam Sandler movie. What can I say? It's not like you need a functioning brain to enjoy that stuff.

A human walked into the room carrying a tray of just-washed glassware. He looked at me for just a second, then averted his eyes as he walked to the counter to set the tray down. It wasn't until he walked out the door that I realized he was wearing a big number thirty-three on his shirt.

"Hey! Wasn't that one of my herd?"

"Huh?" Dr. Joseph turned his head toward the now empty doorway. "Hell, I don't know. They all look alike to me." He scratched his chin—I don't know why... we don't itch—and said, "Could be, though. New people get attached to me all the time once we verify their training and credentials."

"Well, no one told me! I can't afford to lose any more from the engineering program." I shook my head. What the hell was the Council thinking? The answer was, of course, they weren't. As usual, they were just following trends. It didn't matter they had set for me an unrealistic quota to fill. No, they had to go peeling off my prospects to support research that may go nowhere.

I didn't finish my shift. I just stormed out looking for someone to complain to.

***

"Well, *that* didn't go as planned," I snapped as I threw my jacket on the stool next to Bob. The bar was our regular hangout after work. Alcohol did weird things to us after the change. We couldn't get drunk—you need a way to transport it to the brain, after all—but it made the inside of our mouths feel all funny. No taste, just an odd and intense tingling that you could almost hear.

"How's that?"

I sat down on my jacket and waved at the bartender. He grabbed the bottle nearest to him and poured a drink to set it in front of me. Like I said… no taste, so any alcohol is good alcohol to a zombie.

"Council took one of our herd and stuck them with Doc Joseph. I went to the courthouse to bitch about it, but I kept getting the runaround. No one seemed to know who signed the orders."

"Ah," was all he said. Bob wasn't really a type-A personality. He took a sip from his glass and swished it around in his mouth for a while, then spit it back into the glass. Most of us did that. The alcohol was all that mattered, and as long as it hadn't evaporated from the mixture, it was still useful. Me, I found the practice disgusting.

"Yeah, they sent number thirty-three over to him last night."

"Thirty-three? Man, that dude gets around."

"What do you mean?"

"Couple 'a weeks ago I saw him workin' down by the feed lots," he said, staring into his glass.

"Huh…" That was strange. The Council preferred the stock to stay in one discipline once they were tracked. I never heard of one of them working on more than one plan before. "How long have we had the guy in our herd?"

"Hell, I don't know, Jeff," he said around another sip. "Two… three months, maybe?"

"Then why the hell was he off the reservation and down by the feed lots a few weeks back?" That didn't make sense. You get new stock, you keep them, or they are tracked to another program and you never see them again. Or they end up on the table come supper time. Going away and coming back meant they had washed out twice and were only good for food. "Something's hinkey, man."

"Think so?" Bob never turned to me or even set his drink down since I sat on the stool, but he did so now. "What in this great wide world these days ain't?"

I stared at him while I thought that over. Finally, I smiled and said, "Point taken."

"I wouldn't worry about it too much," he said as he turned back to his drink. "I hear we're gettin' another batch soon. Judy said the guy she ate the other day was some kinda scout or somethin'. Patrol found a camp a couple miles north just off 77 near Los Fresnos and rounded 'em all up." He waved the bartender over to refill his glass, and said, "There's s'posed to be about twenty of them, and they're all pretty smart I hear."

"What makes you think they won't get sent to Science?"

"Ah hell, Jeff, even after the outbreak over there, Science is still pretty full up. We're the only group with a major shortage *and* a priority designation. They're comin' our way, friend. Count on it."

Huh. Maybe that's why the Council reassigned number thirty-three. I couldn't recall offhand if he was catching all the material before he left, so he might be a washout after all. Washouts from Engineering didn't usually head over to Science, though.

"Know what's funny?" I turned to look at my friend, sure whatever he said next *wouldn't* be funny.

"What's that?"

"The Patrol leader, Sarah, told me the group was just sittin' there like they were waitin' for somethin'. Didn't even try to run, and barely fought at all." He shrugged, and said, "She said it was like they knew we weren't gonna eat them."

***

Like I said, freezing weather is not our friend. Once humans figured this out, those that were left moved north as fast as they could. Humanity was breeding a whole new crop of Eskimos, but over the last two years they began venturing as far south as the weather would permit. We, though, tended to keep to our narrow band of habitable land. There was no reason to move north, since we would just have to move back in the winter. Humans generally stayed out of our area, mostly because they didn't want to get eaten, but also because getting bitten might spark a new outbreak in their own communities. They could come in with heavy weapons to try to clean us out, but we had our own military-grade weaponry on hand to repel them if needed.

The Mason-Dixon line became a demarcation between Zombie and Human territory. We couldn't cross that line for an extended stay, nor could they. It was a shaky and unspoken detente, since neither side could understand the speech of the other very well. We could still read, but that was a painfully slow way to negotiate.

So you can understand why, during the following two weeks, I pondered over the *why* of sending a lightly armed Human expedition into Zombie territory. It didn't make sense. Worse, the Council didn't seem to care. They were content with simply sending us new stock for the herd.

"There was a *radio* in one of the knapsacks?"

"Short-range, too," Sarah said as she leaned against the wall with me. We were in the exercise yard watching the new stock interact with those I had left from the original herd, listening to their bird-like—to us—voices rising and falling in pitch as they spoke excitedly to one another.

"Did you find another group nearby, then?"

"Nope. Not a sign," she said.

"Curiouser and curiouser," I mused. Sarah was a recent addition to our society. Former Marine, tall and lithe, with an athlete's body and shoulder-length blond hair tied back in a pony tail, she was the kind of woman I would have lusted over in another life. I tried to remember that feeling, and couldn't. Things were much simpler now.

"On a marginally related note, the Council voted last night to begin reproducing."

"You're shittin' me!" This was a strongly debated, and highly controversial move. The community was split right down the middle on this. Our new species couldn't reproduce sexually, so the only option left was to infect Humans. We all remembered enough of our previous lives to be at least a little queasy about the proposition, but this latest Human incursion into our territory must have really spooked the Council.

"Nope, I shit you not. In fact, all those flamethrowers are about to be replaced by goddamn *lassos*," she said as she shook her head. "For the next outbreak, you're supposed to tie them up until the change is complete."

I stood staring at her in stunned silence. This was beyond stupid. How were we supposed to control something like that with such weak tools? It was a disaster waiting to happen.

I was about to comment on this very thing when the sound from the herd suddenly stopped. Gathered in a circle, all facing inward, they were too far away to see what was happening in the center. They soon broke out into loud cheers, then instantly fell silent again as they turned as one to face Sarah and me. We both stepped away from the wall where we were leaning, and she pulled her weapon to the ready. I placed a hand on the barrel to lower it, and the herd slowly dispersed, watching us sideways the whole time.

"That was… odd," she said through tight lips. Her eyes were narrowed, never leaving the herd as each member meandered away from one another.

"Indeed it was," I began, then stopped mid-thought. There, near the center of the group that was drifting apart, was good old number thirty-three. Right in the middle of my goddamn herd. He wasn't facing me, so he didn't see that I noticed he was there.

"What's wrong?" Sarah looked at me, concerned. While zombies don't get sick, we do sometimes have our brains just shut off for no reason. I must have looked like that, so I turned to look her in the eyes.

"There's a human in my herd that shouldn't be there, and it's not the first time he's been someplace he shouldn't."

***

So there I was, on a hunch, laying on a table in Doc Joseph's lab in the middle of the night with a sheet over me and pretending to be a cadaver. It's really easy to do when you don't have to breathe. I even had a toe-tag. Earlier in the day, I found a working Taser at the police station, and held it out of sight close to my leg. They didn't work on zombies—unless you hit us right at the base of the skull, causing us to sing, of all things—but they worked just fine on Humans. I figured I might have to do this several nights in a row before something happened, but I knew it was only a matter of time

I know what you're thinking, but getting the cops involved meant getting the *Council* involved. History showed that was a bad idea. Near as I can tell, almost every decision they've made has been bone-headed. And not just because most of them have chunks of flesh missing from their skulls.

I checked the clock on the wall. Midnight. Magic hour. Humans slept, even if zombies didn't, so I guessed this was the perfect time for the sneaky little bastard to make his move.

I wasn't disappointed.

The door slowly creaked open on hinges begging for oil, and Thirty-Three poked first his head, then the rest of him, into the lab. The lights were off, so he didn't notice me laying there as the door closed behind him. Not until he snapped on the lights and I sat up. Most guys in his position would have pissed their pants, but not Thirty-Three. He froze with his right hand still on the light switch, obviously considering his options. His eyes darted around the room as I swung my legs around and stood up. As his eyes tracked down to the Taser in my hand, his shoulders slumped and he took his hand away from the light switch and stepped fully into the room.

I made no moves toward him—I didn't want him go go rabbit on me. Something about running prey always kicked us into predator mode, and he was smart enough to know that. We don't get superpowers from the change. We're no more athletically gifted than we were before, though we do see better in the dark and our reflexes improve a bit. What we *do* gain, though, is a clarity of purpose. Put live meat in front of us, and a hunger in our bellies, and we will just keep coming at you with everything we have until the job is done. Humans, except in rare instances, can't match that. A human has enough bite force to tear right through skin, muscle, and bone to rip off a finger, but they can't do it because their logical brains say it shouldn't be possible. We don't have that problem.

Turning back to the table, I grabbed a piece of poster board I brought with me. Talking was out of the question, since mostly what he would hear would be a series of grunts and growls that sound almost like language, and I would get mostly the same from him. I held up the board with the words "We need to talk" printed on them in block letters drawn by what was—by all appearances—a palsied third-grader.

He responded by pointing at the whiteboard on the other side of the room. I nodded, and then we both spent the next few minutes searching for a damn marker that wasn't already dried out.

Finally, he wrote "My name is Thomas."

I didn't care. He would always be Thirty-Three to me. Still, I grabbed the marker from him and wrote "I'm Jeff. Now, what the hell are you doing?" I started to hand the marker back, then thought better of it and added, "Don't lie." I then handed him the marker as I gave him a look that reinforced the point.

He stood there watching me for a while, and I was pretty sure he was considering which lie might work and which would get him killed. After a minute or so, he grimaced, shrugged his shoulders and wrote, "I've been working on an inoculation for the disease."

Thought so. Inoculation... not cure. Either he had given up because it wasn't possible, or...

"A cure is pointless now. Most are too damaged to survive a cure. My goal has always been to keep the disease from spreading."

I nodded at that. I had done a pretty good job at protecting myself, but even I was already too far gone to survive a reversal. Newcomers like Sarah might, but they were damn few in number.

"How close are you to perfecting?"

He looked me hard in the eyes, again deciding how best to respond. Then he wrote, "It's done. My last test was a complete success. No new infections."

"Why did you and your team come here for testing?" His eyes grew wide at my leap in logic. Of *course* the new captures were part of a team. They were at least his escorts through enemy territory, if not actual scientists themselves.

"We don't have enough of the Dead left in the North for testing, and we certainly didn't want to test the vaccine on our uninfected there. The humans here are already doomed. We can't mount a rescue, but we can use them to find a solution."

Even I was appalled at this. He might not have it in his power to save them all, but simple humanity required that he try to save *some.* Instead he was using them as guinea pigs.

I think he saw the anger building within me, and he hastily wrote, "All were volunteers. They knew the risks and the situation."

Yeah, right. Lab rats always know what's gonna happen to them. Sure they do. There was something tickling the back of my brain—an idea that was trying to form. I watched him as he watched me, his weight shifting from one foot to the other. I noticed something in his face I hadn't recognized at first, but I remember seeing it in the faces of the herd with which I had seen him interact.

Hope. I remember what hope looked like, and it was all over the faces of the herd.

Suddenly it hit me.

"Is the cure inheritable?"

His eyes grew wide and darted from me to the door. He didn't try to run, though. I gave him points for that.

"No," he wrote at last. "It's actually a retrovirus I created to rewrite our DNA. It can't be inherited," he hesitated before he finished, "but it can be spread."

There it was. In a flash I saw everything laid out like I was watching a documentary. We were finished. Sure, it would take time, but eventually every human would become immune. I laughed at the Council's plans for a "breeding" program. We were now infertile in every sense. Sure, we could still use humans for food, but in less than a decade every one of us will have worn out to the point humans could just walk around us in the street like so many potholes to be avoided.

Maybe it's for the best. Evolution is a harsh bitch, and we were just another failed experiment.

I thought about checking to see if this guy were somehow the "lone scientist" I remembered from every apocalypse-type movie I'd ever seen. You know the one—the only researcher who has the answer. The one no one listens to until all is apparently lost, only to be taken seriously just in time to save the day.

Except real life doesn't work that way. This guy might be the smartest one on the team, but there *was* a team. This kind of research requires lots of people working in lots of specialties. Even if I ate him right now, it was already too late.

***

It turned out to be remarkably easy. There was nearly an hour before daylight when the shifts were supposed to change, and as usual, the next shift was late. I helped Thomas get all his crew out, then we went to work freeing as many of the others as we could. I probably could have gone with them, but they would never feel safe around me. Besides, all my friends are here.

I sat on the steps of the school entrance until Bob showed up. I didn't tell him what happened—only that I arrived early to find the place empty. After he came back outside, he sat on the steps beside me.

"Think the Council will blame us?"

I kept staring north, and snorted. "Count on it," I said.

He turned to look where I was looking and squinted his eyes. There was nothing to see, but he seemed to understand. "Well," he said at last, "since we ain't got no herd to supervise, why don't we head on over to the bar?" He stood, accompanied by the sound of popping joints.

I looked up and said, "It's a little early for drinking, Bob."

"Worried about yer liver?"

I laughed as I put out my hand and he drew me up.

He placed an arm around my shoulder, and then pointed his chin north. "Don't worry 'bout the herd, Jeff. I'm sure they'll be fine." We turned in the direction of the bar, and he said, "Besides, that bunch woulda made lousy engineers. Best they find their own way."

Existence is hard for a zombie, but I felt good for the first time in years. That's when I understood something else. Thomas lied to me. The cure was in my system, now. I didn't know what the end-game would be, but at least my humanity was back.

My son was two, and my wife and I knew we had a preco-
scious child on our hands when he started teaching himself to read.
By the time he was eight, he thought he was fifteen and the wonder
had tarnished a bit. Still, he's likeable enough to inspire this tale.

REQUIEM IN BLUE AND PINK

IT'S ANOTHER GRAY SATURDAY OUTSIDE, THE SUN LITTLE more than a bright argent smear overhead. Inside the gallery, where I sit on what's become *my* bench, the warm artificial light washes over the paintings on the wall before me. This is where I'm most comfortable; and though I spend my first hours each week studying a new work, I always end up here with my two favorites.

"Good afternoon, Billy," Johnny says, settling in beside me.

"Hey, Johnny," I say, returning his greeting without turning my head. Sudden movement in my periphery while I'm focused on a work makes me dizzy. Johnny knows this, and never takes offense at my lack of eye contact. He's older than me, and more traveled, with an odd sense of style. Even this close to Los Angeles, Johnny stands out as a bit flamboyant.

"Sarah joining us today?" he asks. Small for my age, Johnny towers over me even when we're sitting, and I try to ignore him looking over my shoulder. Sarah, like Johnny, is a fixture in the gallery, but she hasn't been here much this month. Honestly, I don't like her hanging around all the time.

I miss her when she's not, though.

"I don't think so. She was pretty upset we ignored her the whole day last time."

"Hmm," is all he says.

I close my eyes to clear the image, then turn to my friend. "I still don't understand the color choices the artist made with this work," I tell him, pointing to the canvas in front of me. "It's so out of place for the period."

Johnny looks at the painting, tilting his head, his shoulder-length brown hair falling to one side. "I've heard he was responding to criticism from a rival painter."

"Ah," I nod. *That* I understand. Tell me something must be a certain way, and I'll go after every scrap of evidence to prove you wrong. I do that with my mom all the time. I look at my Jordans, laces untied and flopping as I swing my legs. "I've been thinking about 'William'."

Johnny smiles. We've discussed this many times since he first suggested it.

"About time, Bill... um, *William*. You're going on ten, now. Much too old for such a cutesy name," he says, and leans toward me. "Maybe now you'll call me Jonathan."

He knows I can't. Words and sounds carry more than just meaning for me. I associate some of them with tastes and smells. "Johnny" is okay, as far as odors go, but "Jonathan" is pure dog poop. I can't even think the name without getting a whiff.

I smile, wrinkling my nose. "Daddy thinks it's silly, but Mom seems to like it." Mom doesn't smile much anymore. Her smile smells like honey and lemon—my favorites—so I take every opportunity to make it happen.

Johnny sighs, opens his mouth to speak, then stops. The silence feels like a heavy coat around my shoulders, rough wool and scratchy. He's always careful with his words, and I appreciate the consideration. Sometimes, though, the silence is worse.

"Are you going through with it?" he says without looking at me.

I continue to swing my legs. The breeze it stirs sounds like a lullaby, and is just as calming.

"Yeah," I say, still watching my feet. "Daddy thinks the gene therapy will fix the part of my DNA controlling my condition." I take a shuddering breath, refusing to look Johnny in the eye. "He says it's not a cure, though. My brain is hard-wired now, but he thinks the treatment will keep it from getting worse."

"Sensory overload," he says with a nod.

"Yeah," I nod back. *Synesthesia.* The word tastes funny, but Daddy is a geneticist and he explained it to me. I am one of the rare fivefold variety, with each of my major senses tied to the others in ways that cause endless variations of connections. I taste and smell sounds, numbers are all connected in space, and touch becomes colors and shapes in my head. Sounds translate to colors, feeling, and motion. Mom calls me special, but what she means is *different*. It drips from her voice like old engine oil, thick and black.

I've known I was different from the other kids since my first day of public school; the bullying began the day Miss Purkey praised my artwork in front of the class. I had been painting from the age of two when I toddled into Mom's studio and grabbed a brush while she wasn't looking. The still life she was working on wasn't right, so I fixed it. Of course the colors I chose were all wrong, she said, but she gave me an easel and my own supplies. The truth is, I never paint pictures. I paint *sound.* Natural sounds work fine, but music is by far the best.

One warm Sunday afternoon we were each beginning a new work, Strauss' *Die Fledermaus* playing softly in the background, and Mom said the music distracted her. When

I came home from school two days later, a smaller studio waited for me in the back yard. I knew the music wasn't the real reason—she was jealous because my art was selling and hers was not. That was the first time I remember Mom and Daddy arguing. It was loud, and it hurt so bad I ran to my room and huddled under my bed. They found me there with my fists over my ears to block out the noise.

"Well, I think it's stupid!" Sarah's voice, coming from over my shoulder, smells like a campfire gone out of control. It's as startling as she intends, and the light in the room changes to a deep red. My hands cover my ears on reflex, but I pull them away at once.

"Nobody asked you!" Johnny always intercedes on my behalf. He knows I can't raise my voice in anger.

"He'll remake you, Billy. Change you into something you're not and were never intended to be." She walks around to sit beside me, opposite Johnny, dark hair beneath her Easter hat framing a heart-shaped face. Her pink dress flutters as she sits, and she smooths the fabric against her legs with delicate hands. "This is how you were born, Billy," she says, her voice thick and sweet, "and it's what is special about you. It's not a *defect* that needs some kind of conversion therapy." She pats my leg, a comforting rhythm. "Those methods— along with their brutality— were discredited years ago."

"His name's *William*, now, in case you weren't paying attention," Johnny sneers.

Sarah laughs, twin bells jingling in the air. "See what I mean? Everyone keeps trying to change you." She lays a hand over mine. "It's the differences that make us special," she says. "Your mom should know that. You don't have to be like everyone else to be normal."

"Don't listen to her, William," Johnny shoots back, more at her than me. "She doesn't understand."

"That's enough, guys." If I allow this to go on, the whole day will be wasted—my mental canvas covered in crap. I stand and turn to address them both. "Daddy understands my condition better than anyone, and I trust him," I say, wagging a finger in their faces, but even I have trouble believing.

"And what of us?" Sarah's eyes are soft and fearful, and closer to tears than I ever remember seeing them.

I shrug my shoulders, then look at my feet. "I don't know, Sarah." Daddy is staring at me from his usual spot in the doorway. "Gotta go," I say, grabbing my sketchbook and pencils and shoving them into my pack. "See you guys next week, 'kay?"

Sarah looks at me with a tilt of her head, then at my Daddy. He takes no notice of her—he never does—and waves me over. "Sure, Billy," she says to my back. "We'll be here."

"Aren't we always?" Johnny adds with a shrug and a lopsided smile.

***

I toss my pack on the bench in the entryway. The drive had been quiet, allowing me to focus without the usual burden on my senses. Daddy is good about that, but I know as soon as I walk in the house, Mom will bombard me with questions about my day. She's nervous about the procedure, and I can taste her fear in every word. I hit the stairs at a run, hoping to make it to my room before she realizes we're home.

"Dinner will be ready soon, guys," she calls from the kitchen.

I sigh, stopping on the third step, and ask on autopilot "What are we having?"

"Chicken and rice."

Of course it is. It's almost always chicken and something. Mom knows it's the one thing that doesn't taste like anything else, so she serves it every chance she gets. There are only so many ways to prepare chicken though.

"Janet, that boy's gonna wake up crowing at the morning sun if you feed him any more chicken," Daddy says from behind me at the door. There's a pained smile on his face as he shrugs off his jacket.

She walks into the foyer, shoes tapping against the marble tile, and eyes us both as she dries her hands with a towel. "Next time you guys can choose," she says, her mouth tight and sour. "I promise I won't complain." She holds us with a look, turns on her heels, and walks back to the kitchen without another word. Daddy doesn't notice the army of crabs clicking along in her wake.

"I guess we better get washed up," he says. He tosses his keys on the little table by the door and hangs his jacket on the hook above it, then takes his first hesitant steps down the little hall toward the kitchen. He keeps shoving his hands into his pockets and pulling them out like he doesn't know what to do with them. No crabs follow, only a sick yellow fog rolling at his feet like swamp water.

I climb the stairs, hoping to get to my room and close the door before the argument begins.

***

We eat in near silence, our plastic utensils making little noise as they scrape against the plastic plates. Mom abandoned her fine china and silverware the first time I told her what they sounded like. I think it frightened her to know *those* pictures were in my head. I swing my legs as I eat, allowing the light breeze to evoke a gentle music. The chicken is as bland as I knew it would be, but the rice contains hints of garlic and butter that are, for once, not unpleasant.

"Your father tells me you're working on something new, sweetheart. What's the subject?" Mom never goes into my studio anymore. She rarely even looks at my work, but is always curious, each time asking about the "subject" though, which is dumb. I don't do *subjects*.

"It's a commissioned piece for the lobby in one of the Dupont offices," I tell her. Mouth tight as she listens, her head tilts a shallow angle to show interest. "I'm using the Hindemith *Symphonic Metamorphosis* for inspiration, if that means anything."

Daddy is watching me, eyes narrow and wary. He's a scientist, and never understands our conversations about art, but he sees a fight brewing.

Mom places her knife and fork down and joins her hands in front of her on the table. "That's a bit... *heroic*, don't you think? I mean, for a lobby."

I sigh in true dramatic fashion. "*Third* movement, Mom," I say, rolling my eyes. "Not the March."

"Ah," is all she says, and picks up her utensils, attacking the bird with dainty fingers. She stabs a small piece of breast meat, draws it to her mouth, and pauses. Raising an eyebrow, she says, "Painting about music is like dancing about architecture, you know." Satisfied, she finishes the motion and chews in silence.

"Martin Mull," I tell her. "Though that's a bastardization of the original quote, '*Talking* about music is like dancing about architecture.'"

For a heartbeat, she freezes. Then she slams both hands on the table on either side of her plate, rattling everything. What I see is a miniature fireworks display over the table. It's kind of pretty, and I smile on reflex.

"You think it's *funny* to use that language at the dinner table?"

"No, Mom! I didn't mean..." I stammer.

"Janet," Daddy says, reaching across the table to place his hand gently atop hers, "I don't think he was being disrespectful." He looks at me sideways, but keeps his face toward Mom. "It's just that he remembers everything he's ever read." He turns and nods at me. "Right, son?" he says to me, his eyes pleading.

I take the hint. "That's right, Mom. I didn't mean anything by it."

She pulls her hands from his, places them in her lap, and turns to face Daddy. "You and that boy are always ganging up on me, Charles. Is it any wonder he has no respect for me?"

"No one's ganging up on you, sweetheart." He looks only at her, dismissing me from the conversation. "This isn't about his behavior, though."

"I don't want to talk about it," she says as she shakes her head. She's still staring at her plate, the food an afterthought now. She gathers her things and pushes away from the table to stand. "I've had enough," she says to her food, and walks toward the kitchen. Daddy looks at me, his mouth a thin line, eyes narrowed, and nods toward Mom.

"I'm sorry, Mom," I call after her.

She stops, shoulders relaxing. "It's okay, William," she says without turning. Another deep breath, and she leaves the room.

Once she's gone, Daddy turns his face back to me, pushing his glasses up the bridge of his long nose. I know he's counting to ten in his head, and I'm forced to recite the first ten prime numbers in mine.

"Why do you *do* that?" he asks, leaning across the table. His chair creaks, an eagle screeching as it swoops over the table.

My face is hot. I have no answer. We finish our meal in silence, accompanied by the sounds of Mom cleaning the kitchen like a Roman legion going into battle. After I go to my room, the real fight begins below. It's my fault. It's *always* my fault. The air around me gets hotter, and I try to distract myself with Eric Whitacre's *Sleep*.

It doesn't help.

***

The table is cold, and every time I touch it I hear a marching band playing in the distance. By my third treatment, Daddy is bringing my favorite blanket for me to sit on. It's soft and fuzzy, and I've had it since they first brought me home from the hospital. Daddy has been trying to separate me from it for years, but Mom keeps rescuing it from the donation pile. As he spreads it on the table, he hums a tune that might be Don McLean's *American Pie*. I could be wrong; Daddy can't carry a tune in a bucket.

"The doctor should be here in a minute," he says while he works. He always says that. I don't know why. I have yet to visit a doctor who keeps their appointment time, the understanding being that their time is more valuable than mine. They're wrong, of course. These days, no single doctor can afford to commission one of my works.

"How many more do I need?" I'm not whining, and he knows it. The treatments are expensive, and even though Daddy works in the field, his connections only go so far.

"We've been over this, son," he says as he helps me onto the table. "Even if it works, you will need at least a few more before we are sure." He stops fussing and looks me in the eyes. "There's also the probability you will need regular treatments for the rest of your life," he says. Seeing the look on my face, he adds before I can complain, "But those will be annual treatments at the very worst."

Just as I start to protest, Dr. Mengele opens the door and steps in. That's not really his name, but it's the one I use in my head.

"Hey, doc," I say. "We're just talking about how much you're gonna get paid over the next twenty years." He stops for only a second, and then smiles at me and Daddy.

"Nice to see you, too, Billy." He flips through my chart—an obvious pretense at study since he already knows my case well. He pulls the little rolling stool over to the table and sits, using his otoscope to check my ears and eyes, whistling tunelessly the whole time. "Have you noticed any effects from the treatments yet?"

I look at Daddy, and he nods, an encouraging smile on his face. "I'm not sure... but doctor's exams *seem* less annoying now," I deadpan. The doctor raises an eyebrow at me, then turns to Daddy.

Daddy gives me a pained look, and says, "His color choices in his artwork are more natural, now." He hesitates a second before adding, "At least his mother thinks so."

I draw a short breath; I hadn't even noticed the change. It scares me to think my art might become average. *Pedestrian.*

"What about sounds?"

"I still get colors, if that's what you mean," I say. "But they're not as... um... saturated, I guess is the best description."

He straightens and rolls back a foot or two. "Multiply three-thousand twenty-one and fourteen thousand fifty-three."

As he reads the numbers from his pad, I close my eyes and watch the digits form and connect in my mind. "Forty-two million, four hundred fifty-four thousand, one hundred and... um... thirteen." I look at Daddy. "I think."

The doctor studies me and narrows his eyes, "Numbers still spatially sequenced?"

"Yeah, but the connecting lines are thinner and less distinct." My head hurts.

He rubs his chin, then turns to Daddy. "I think we're seeing a bit more progress than expected. I don't want to get your hopes up"—he tilts his head, and looks at me—"either of you... but with just a few more treatments we should see some major improvement."

"Are you talking fully cured?" Daddy asks. His eyes are wide, and his breathing heavy. "His mother will be pleased, of course, but—"

"Charles, you know better than anyone that's not possible. I *am* talking about the possibility of a normal life though."

Normal? I think. What is normal, anyway? I look at my Daddy. He's right, Mom *will* be pleased. All she ever wants is for me to be normal. The same as everyone else.

The same as her.

Daddy is smiling, and his eyes are moist. Before I can process any of it, he gathers me up and hugs me so hard my chest hurts.

***

With Alfred Reed's *Russian Christmas Music* blaring at full volume, I stand in my studio in front of a large white canvas. I always play the Reed when I get stuck. The last four minutes of the piece work as mental drain cleaner, clearing the unnecessary and useless pictures.

Today, though, even the glory of the horns fails me. By the end of the recording I notice I'm crying, shocked to realize it's because of the beauty of the music rather than the pictures I normally see. The canvas, in fact, is still a stark white, unmarred by a single stroke of my brush. I reach up with my free hand and rub the side of my head. The pain has grown worse over the past month, so bad that some days it's all I can do to just crawl out of bed. Even sunlight hurts.

A light rap at the door grabs my attention. Mom stands in the opening, hesitating at the threshold. She steps into my studio on silent feet, her eyes locking on the blank canvas.

"Still having trouble?"

"Yeah, a little." I don't know what else to say. It's the longest I've ever been stuck, and the look on her face isn't helping.

"Why don't you step away from it for a while, honey," she says, her voice soft and reassuring. "I've always found time off helps."

"I have a deadline, Mom."

"Self-imposed," she shoots back. "And I'm only suggesting a break."

I look at the canvas again, then the brush in my hand. *Why is there yellow paint on it? There's no yellow in this piece.*

"Yeah," I say, and set the brush down. "Maybe you're right."

Her lopsided smile matches the tilt of her head. "Of course I'm right," she says. "I'm Mom."

Hooking her arm in mine, she leads me toward the door. I look into her eyes and notice we are almost the same height. *When did that happen?*

"What did you have in mind?"

She smiles at me and says, "How does a movie sound?"

"As long as it has nothing to do with snow," I say. "I've stared at enough white for one day."

She laughs at that, and for once it sounds... just *pretty.*

***

"Mom and Daddy took me to Disneyland last week for my birthday. I think they were trying to cheer me up after the disastrous showing last month." Jonathan and Sarah stand without comment, listening to me ramble for the past half hour. They speak infrequently now. "Mom's happier, and she smiled a lot at Disneyland. Yesterday she said she would teach me proper color mixing and how to choose a palette." Both my friends are angry with me, but I can't help that. "Daddy's been happier, too. I think it's just because Mom smiles more often." My head hurts all the time now—sometimes so bad I sit in my room with the lights out and cry—but Mom and Daddy no longer fight. I don't know if that's a fair trade, but it's the one I made.

The Huntington is unusually quiet today, and not just because my friends aren't speaking to me. I am accustomed to all the sounds of the building, both natural and mechanical, that used to elicit colors and odors. Now there's none of that. It was the same when we went to Disneyland, and was the first time I'd ever braved such a mass of sights, sounds, and smells without being overwhelmed. My favorite part was the parade, and once we were home, I ran straight to my studio to capture the lights and sounds on canvas. After a few hours I surrendered in frustration. Even the music didn't help.

"Daddy's taking me to the park later. He says it's time I learned to throw a proper spiral." Nothing. Not even a smirk at the thought of me trying to throw a football. I want my friends to be happy for me, but they can't and I know why. Sarah clammed up weeks before Jonathan did, but soon even he stopped talking. I shrug and sigh at the loss. Daddy appears in the doorway and I force a smile. "I guess it's time to go," I say, gathering my things and running to my father to give him a hug. I turn back to wave goodbye to my friends. They stand in stoic silence, both posed in casual indifference.

We all know I can't come back.

JIMMY

I WAS TWELVE THE LAST TIME I SAW JIMMY CROSS. THE SKY was an achingly clear cerulean blue, a typical December day on the Texas Gulf Coast, and I waved goodbye as he flew away. I pretended he waved back, but he was too far away by then, and the sleek metal tube in which he rode didn't have much in the way of windows, anyway. I held to that illusion with tight fists, and over the years I embellished the memory, polishing it like a gemstone to where I even saw him smile as he waved.

It's funny what we can make ourselves believe sometimes.

The man sitting across from me now isn't Jimmy. At least, not the Jimmy from my childhood. So much changes in forty-plus years. For starters, this Jimmy smokes. That summer before he left for good, we attempted to smoke one of my daddy's Camels I lifted from his pocket. We ran to the field behind Jimmy's house, confident the tall grass and weeds hid us from the ever-present gaze of our parents. Even before my daddy caught us, we swore never to try that again. It took ten minutes to catch our breath after the first puff.

"Got a light?" Jimmy held the cigarette across the table—Camel unfiltered—and the manacles around his wrists clanked tonelessly. "C'mon, Chris," he smiled warmly, his eyes twinkling. "Cut a guy some slack." He waved the dry paper tube in the air like a wand, and said, "You gotta light, or not?"

I pointed to the NO SMOKING sign over his shoulder, not even bothering to ask where he got the cancer stick. The guard behind me at the door snorted.

Jimmy flicked the cigarette onto the table in mild disgust and settled back in his seat, dropping his hands to his lap. Jimmy was always the "cool one", and even now, in the most uncomfortable straight-back chairs in the known world, he managed a calmly aloof near-relaxation. James Dean couldn't have done it any better.

I pressed the red button on the digital micro-recorder and set it on the table. "For the record, state your full name."

Jimmy sniffed, raising one eyebrow in my direction. I wasn't fooled. Minutes ago he was checking every inch of the room with calm detachment. He was buying time as he planned his escape. It didn't help that we both knew he would probably succeed.

"For the record," he drawled, leaning toward the recorder, "my full given name is James Steven Cross." He flopped back again as he finished.

"Can you explain your presence at a secure government facility last night?"

"Can you?" He all but sneered.

"I'm not the one in irons," I said, tilting my head toward his shackles. "Please answer the question."

He shrugged and frowned. "I came to see you, Chris."

"Me," I said without inflection. I had his statement from the initial interrogation in front of me, but it didn't hurt to have him repeat everything for the sake of consistency.

"We have to go back, Chris." He leaned forward, elbows on the table, and the guard stiffened. "Chill out, Captain America," he said to the guard. "Don't get all twitchy." Sergeant Dietrich pinned Jimmy to the chair with a steely gaze but did not relax his stance.

"Back?" I said, guiding the conversation back on track.

"To where it all began. Where things got all screwed up."

"I don't follow."

"Chris," he began, a wan smile on his lips as he shook his head, "it was never supposed to be me. You have to know that, right?"

I didn't know what he meant, but I knew with certainty where it all began. Right before my twelfth birthday in the summer of '72.

***

"Hey Chris—how about this one?" Jimmy tossed another beautiful hunk of junk from inside the greasy old dumpster behind Hellman Ford. Sunday was a great day for picking through their auto shop trash.

I bent over and snagged it from where it landed in the dirt. "Looks like an old carburetor or something," I said, picking off the dried leaves and rocks. "It'll do," I added, then tossed it in the woogedy old wheelbarrow we used to transport our rocket parts.

Jimmy grabbed the rim of the dumpster and vaulted out, sticking the landing like a gymnast. "Got a good haul, today," he said, looking at the pile of metal, wire, and Bakelite. "Let's get it back to Mission Control."

We took turns with the wheelbarrow, navigating the alley between the dealership and our neighborhood. The only hard part was getting it through Jimmy's gate in the rusty chain-link fence. From deep inside Jimmy's house,

81

his older brother Trey was belting out an off-key rendition of Bill Withers' "Lean on Me".

"Probably should close the windows when he does that," I said, snickering.

"Ain't that the truth," Jimmy said, struggling to pull the wheelbarrow through the weeds choking the gate. "Hey," he said, bending to pull something from the tangle, "check it out!"

What he showed me was an expended rocket someone shot off two days ago on the Fourth. The thing was a foot long and an inch or more in diameter. The nosecone was still attached, but the long stick used to anchor it was broken off near the business end. The white paper covering the tube was dirty, but the word Longhorn was still visible in all its colorful glory.

"Cool," I said, snatching it from his hand. "Maybe we can use this as a booster or something."

Not one of my better ideas.

Getting Trey to help was worse.

"I've got some Black Cats left," Trey said that afternoon. Fifteen, tall, and with a curly shock of dirty blond hair, he was the quintessential older brother with a twisted sense of humor, and his Cheshire cat grin should have tipped us off. "We can open 'em up and pour them in the tube for rocket fuel."

"How many do we need?" Jimmy asked, neither of us suspecting anything.

"Oh," Trey said, turning the thing over in his hands like an engineer tackling a problem, "I figure a hundred or so should do it."

So the three of us carefully broke open the last of Trey's stash of firecrackers and poured the black powder into the tube, filling it almost to the end. Trey tied together a dozen or so discarded fuses "for safety," and then sealed everything up with hot paraffin. We commandeered a four-foot length of iron pipe from their father's scrap pile, and I held a brick against one open end as Jimmy held the other up like an anti-aircraft gun.

I should have known something was up when Trey backed away, covering his ears after lighting the fuse.

The explosion was deafening, so we couldn't hear Trey laughing as he rolled on the ground holding his stomach.

Jimmy was yelling and trying to stand, but he also grinned like a madman as he pointed to the perfectly formed smoke ring drifting lazily up and over the neighborhood. It was hours before we got our hearing back.

***

A few days later Trey and his friend David pulled a ratty old canvas off his dad's Rambler parked in the alley behind our clubhouse. The car was furiously rusting in its repose, no amount of protection from the tarp proof against the moldy Gulf Coast atmosphere.

"What do you think, Trey?" David said, grinning sideways. "Can they use this for a parachute for re-entry?"

Trey looked it over while Jimmy and I watched, and he nodded. "Sure. Why not?" He pointed to his father's work shed and said to Jimmy, "Go get some rope."

Jimmy smiled, already forgetting the marvelous debacle of the previous week, and ran to the shed to retrieve the rope. Heavy hemp, and thicker than my thumb.

Together we tied multiple knots at each corner, then Trey fashioned a makeshift harness with the four free ends. He looked around, then up at the old tallow tree near our common fence. "One of you," nodding at Jimmy, "should test it."

David snickered under his hand, but Jimmy just smiled, grabbed the parachute and climbed the tree. Both of us were skilled climbers, but Jimmy got higher than I thought possible. The branch he inched out on bent dangerously under the weight. His eyes were wide as he looked down, but he held steady.

"C'mon," Trey yelled up. "We don't have all day."

Jimmy saluted once, stepped out over open space, and like the cartoon Coyote he seemed to hover for just an instant before falling.

I swear, the damn tarp hit the ground before Jimmy did, square on his ass like a hundred pound sack of flour. He toppled to his side and lay still.

"Oh shit, oh shit, oh shit..." Trey babbled as he ran to his brother. David stayed where he was, silent for the first time since I had known him.

"Are you okay?" I said.

Other than a wheezing struggle to breathe, Jimmy didn't move for a long time. Behind me, David now laughed like a maniac, and soon we were all laughing along with him. Except for Jimmy, of course. It was all he could do to just draw a breath, but the smile on his face was genuine. He always seemed to take these things in stride.

***

"Hurt like hell," he said, rubbing his chest, "but I felt more alive in that two-second drop than any time in my life since."

I looked at my old friend, puzzled. "What did you say?" There were a thousand great memories from that summer. How did he know which one I chose?

And why, after over forty years, does he look like a twenty-year-old?

***

A few months later the bottom dropped out for my generation.

"Did you see it?" Jimmy ran into my house without knocking. None of us ever knocked, and no one ever locked their doors.

"See what?"

"It's all over the news! Some Arab assholes just killed a bunch of the athletes at the Olympics." He said it ay-rab, like everyone else in Texas. "I think they said they were Palestinians or somthin'."

"No way," I said, not wanting to believe him. No one did stuff like that. They were just athletes. Not politicians, or military, or any of the other thousands of functionaries making life miserable for the Palestinians—just normal people going about their daily lives. And it was all captured on television, thrust into our living rooms and our collective psyche. I folded onto the nearby sofa, still in shock. A distant cousin of mine was supposed to be there in Munich, competing in the Summer Games.

"Turn your set on. Cronkite's on right now."

We watched in silence for hours, the world spinning around me as I tried to process the events. Earnest news anchors gave us the basics, leaving our imagination to fill in the horrors. Shaky footage taken with a long lens of the apartments with a lone hostage-taker standing in the window, a German policeman twenty feet away. At one point, an image of a man shouting and being dragged away filled the screen. The reporter said the cops captured him on the scene not long before the attack, trying to break in to the compound. He claimed he was there to stop the terrorists.

"Dude looks like your Uncle Al," Jimmy said.

I leaned closer to the massive Magnavox console. "Kinda does, don't he?" Except for the cap. Uncle Al never wore hats.

***

"Do you know what a Black Swan Event is, Chris?"

The non sequitur prodded me out of my reverie. "Not offhand, no." Sergeant Dietrich shifted his weight and sighed.

Jimmy ignored him. "Occasionally something happens everyone knows is impossible, but since it happened, it must have been possible all along, so society makes up stories after the fact to explain it or fill in the knowledge gaps." He grinned. "Sort of the opposite of science."

"You're talking about religion."

"In a way, yeah. That's how most of them started." He tilted his head again. "One in particular."

Jimmy and me were terrible Baptists as kids. His mom liked to call us her little heathens when she managed to drag us to Sunday service. Most times we'd sit there and try to keep from laughing. Of course, that just made things worse. It wasn't long before our humor shifted to the sermon. I developed a healthy skepticism that year.

"What did you mean earlier about going back?"

"You were the dreamer, Chris," he said with a grin, looking through me to somewhen else. "Smarter, too." The corners of his mouth fell, and his eyes lost their twinkle. "I've tried to learn everything—be the one they need me to be, but I'm just not the right guy." He shrugged and frowned. "All that 'save the world' crap was your bag—not mine, dig?" His fingers made an abortive move toward the discarded cigarette, then curled inward. "Now look at you," he nodded first to me, and then my cap where it lay near the cigarette. "Blue dress uniform and scrambled eggs on your cap." He shook his head. "Not what I pictured for you when we were kids."

"No, Jimmy, I guess not," I said, patience thinning. I leaned forward, the slight height advantage of my chair allowed me to look down on him. "If you could just finish your statement about why you are here, we can move this along."

"*That's* what I'm talkin' about, Chris," he said, pushing himself back in his seat. "This," he waved his arms up and down in front of me, "is not who you were meant to be."

"And just who is it I was supposed to be?"

He tilted his head a tick, and raised an eyebrow, "Well... *me*, I guess.

***

I always wanted to be Jimmy. From as early as I can recall, he was better in almost every category that mattered to a boy. Not just better than me though... he was better than *everyone*. He also knew his limitations. Dreaming was my thing, so for planning our adventures I was often in charge. We were a matched set. Yin and Yang. Castor and Pollux.

Reed Richards and Ben Grimm.

"I know Project Blue Book was dead and buried while we were still kids, but now you're heading up Blue Sky, right?" It wasn't a question.

I felt Sergeant Dietrich smirking over my shoulder. What good Air Force man wouldn't? Blue Book was a running joke... among those who didn't know better. Blue Sky, on the other hand, was known among only a very few in the whole of the federal government.

I kept my face as neutral as I could, but he threw me and we both knew it. I turned to Dietrich and cocked my head. "What's your security clearance, Sergeant?"

His head shifted from the prisoner slightly, eyes never leaving the target. "Top Secret, sir."

I sighed. "Not good enough, I'm afraid." I nodded toward the door.

He opened his mouth to protest, thought better of it, then unholstered his sidearm and placed it on the table by my hand. He turned and left, the only sound of his passing was the heavy door closing softly behind him.

I turned back to my old friend while I gathered up the recorder and switched it off. Only well-worn sorrow marked that face, with a hint of boredom, and not a trace of the road map that comes with age. "What's your point, Jimmy?"

"Just that you are uniquely qualified to hear what I have to say."

"And that is...?"

Jimmy smiled, but not with humor; the corners of his mouth barely lifted. "There's a Great Filter approaching for humanity—the tenth or eleventh, I can't remember for sure—and I'm supposed to lead you past it." He dropped his gaze to the table. "At least that was what they trained me to do." He looked up again. "But like I said, Chris... I'm not the guy."

"Great Filter?"

"Natural stopping points on a species' journey to sentience and eventual galactic colonization. The first Great Filter was having the right type of star with planets in the habitable zone. Another was when simple amino acids formed and then joined to form protein chains. At each point, one little thing goes wrong, and, poof, no life."

"You're talking about Fermi's Paradox." Again... neutral.

Jimmy smiled with one side of his mouth. "As a species gets past each one, they get closer to the point where their own actions become their next Great Filter. Nazi Germany was one. The rise of global terrorism was another." He shook his head. "And they come closer together, sometimes in bunches."

"We've passed all of those, though."

"But humanity's ability to destroy itself is growing exponentially, Chris. If you are *very* lucky, you'll pass the next three or four, and enter a quiet period that may last up to a million years."

I crossed my arms. "And you would know this, how?"

"The guys who took me twelve years ago are coming up on their next Great Filter after over a million years of relative ease."

***

I remember the guys who took Jimmy.

For nearly twelve days in December the two of us, NASA's final stalwarts, watched Apollo 17 begin and complete its mission. It was the last one, but we still didn't know that. No one else in the house even bothered to ask us for updates. Spaceflight was now routine and boring—Apollo 13 already a distant memory. The truth was—for me—after the events in September, the space program no longer held any joy. What was the point? We were all going to kill ourselves, anyway.

Walking the fields behind our neighborhood in sullen silence, we were a mile or more from home that Sunday before the Apollo program's final splashdown.

"What's that?" Jimmy said, pointing at something flashing between the tall weeds.

I started to say I didn't have a clue, but the sudden pain in my head stopped me. I put my hand to my head and dropped to one knee on the damp ground. The rain from the night before cleared before midnight, and today's sky was bright enough to cause a headache all by itself. This, though, wasn't just a headache. I heard music... bells... playing as the pain faded.

"Did you hear that?" I said, trying to stand.

"Hear what?" Jimmy wasn't really listening as he staggered forward. Before I got to my feet he was running, and I struggled to stand and follow. Even on my best day I couldn't keep up with him, and if he hadn't stumbled on a rock, I never would have caught him.

"Why are you running?" I said, stopping beside him trying to catch my breath.

He stood, brushed his knees. "I don't know, Chris."

From somewhere behind us a voice boomed, "Hold up, guys."

When we turned my Uncle Al was barreling though the high grass at a run. Only he wasn't my uncle. Even with his cap pulled down so far, I could see that. Jimmy and I both realized it at the same time and took off toward the bright reflection we saw earlier. I don't know why we ran that way, but the music was still in my head. We broke through into a large circular clearing, a strange silver tube—big as a tanker truck—resting in the center. There was a hole in the side, black as night, but no sign of a door or hatch.

"Stop!" The man was closer now, and Jimmy was ahead, halfway between the tube and the edge of the clearing. Before I could catch him, the man grabbed my arm and held me tight. "Don't. It's not safe." He yelled at Jimmy, "Come back, son."

The tube wasn't touching the ground, instead hovering six or seven inches above the flattened grass and weeds. Jimmy bent to look, then turned back and smiled, and the things inside the tube reached for him out of the blackness.

***

"They're not the first to get to their level, but they might be the first to move past it." His face screwed up for a second, and he looked far away. "When they reached this quiescent period, they thought their trials were behind them. Their species colonized the galaxy, but in their desire to avoid any more filter events, they held back every other civilization on the edge of interstellar travel. Some they watched as the Great Filter swallowed them up, others they nudged down the wrong path."

I stayed quiet. I remember the ship, the... *things* reaching out, Jimmy screaming as they pulled him inside, my best friend screaming for me to help, those red taloned claws gripping his arms, the monster's barbed tail whipping side to side. The man who looked so much like my Uncle Al holding me back while demons pulled Jimmy inside and the hole melted and closed.

"They came to realize there was a new filter in their path, and the only way past it was with help." He looked up into my eyes, pleading. "They need us, Chris. Humanity. We're the first to get this far since they stopped interfering. They need us to join them, passing our tests to become what they are so they can move forward."

I was breathing hard, my face flushed. "But they're still interfering, aren't they?"

"*Nudging,*" he admitted, hesitating slightly. A tiny bead of sweat formed at his temple.

***

"The right man, in the right place, at the right time can make a world of difference." They would not let me go. It was written in the body language all around the conference table... save one. Dr. Wells shared my views, but she was one voice among many. Everyone always brought up the grandfather paradox, or quantum branching, but her math demonstrated the first was a progressively flattening ripple rather than a tsunami. The second either didn't happen or was irrelevant from the observer's point of view.

And observation was all that interested them. Not change.

The chairman looked around at the other five members of the committee. "We'll take it under advisement."

Advisement. Government-speak for *bury it until the next Congress.* Kicking the can down the road didn't affect the program in any meaningful sense, save that the honor of the first trip would fall to someone other than myself.

***

"Take me with you," Jimmy said.

"Where?"

"Wrong question, Chris," he said. "The real question is *when.*"

"I don't know what—"

"Or just go yourself. It doesn't matter who goes, only that *one* of us does."

I stared back at him for a long time. He knew more than he should. How or why didn't matter, but he could seriously muck things up if he continued to open his mouth. The truth was I *did* plan on taking that first trip. There was a wrong that needed righting, and I'd deal with the consequences when—or if—I got back.

"There's nothing to discuss, Jimmy. You aren't going anywhere with me. Once I get up from this table, I'll go back to work, and you'll go to prison."

"Fine," he said without hesitation. "Just fix this, okay?"

"Fix what?"

He slammed his fists on the table, the chains between them rattling noisily and the cigarette danced. "Haven't you been listening?" He shook his head, his shaggy hair whipping his face. "Look at me, Chris," he said, leaning forward, hissing. "They... *did* things to me. For twelve goddamn *years*," his voice rose in both tenor and volume. "But even after all that time and all the training, I'm still not the guy. You have to fix this! It's supposed to be *you* that saves the world... not me."

"How...?" Relativity. Over forty years for me, but only twelve for him. Twelve long, lonely, horror-filled years.

"They don't like time travel. They say the effects are too unpredictable—something about a causality loop—but this is such a *small* change." He looked up at me, eyes pleading. "Just go back and make sure you get to the ship before I do."

Talons... reaching for me. Twelve years. The sickeningly sweet smell coming from the hole in the ship.

Oh God, the smell. Like rotting flesh.

The barbed tail caressing my neck...

"No!" I don't remember standing *or* grabbing the gun. But I can't forget the look of shock and betrayal on

Jimmy's face, hands shielding his head as I squeezed the trigger and splashed his brains along the back wall.

***

The investigation was short. Even though the prisoner was shackled, no one questioned my story. He lunged at me and I was in fear for my life. I was a hero for taking out a would-be terrorist. Or so they said.

It helped that the events involved a facility so secure even the President didn't know about it.

"Are you ready?" Dr. Wells looked up at me, then toward the waiting portal. *They'll arrest her soon, but that will be fixed in the past.* I hoped, at least.

"Ready as I'll ever be," the sound of guards cutting through the door behind me almost drowning out my historic words.

She reached up and kissed me on the cheek. Warm, it promised more should things have turned out differently. *Maybe they will.* Instead I grinned at her, tipped my gimme cap, shoved my hands into my worn-out jeans, and strode toward the portal.

First, I'll go to Munich. After that, I'll stop both of us from getting on the ship.

I'll fix it all this time, Jimmy. I promise.

SLEEPERS

March 24, 2015

NO MATTER WHAT ANYONE SAYS, JET-LAG IS REAL. THE jet-lag experienced traveling from Kazakhstan to Atlanta, Georgia was the worst in Jack Montgomery's opinion. Arriving too late to check in at the CDC, he took a cab the twenty-five miles to his single†††bedroom apartment outside of Sandy Springs. By the time he unlocked his door and tossed his bag and briefcase on the battered leather sofa, it was 2 am and all he wanted to do was fall into bed and sleep for a week. The case bounced once, fell to the floor and spilled its contents. Two pages of his preliminary report stared up at him, peeking from the pile of papers. Both pages were photographs of children asleep in their hospital beds. Round angelic faces poking from beneath slim covers, some clutching fuzzy stuffed animals. Asleep for nearly three months, they were among the first of those suffering from "encephalopathy of unknown etiology"—otherwise known as "we haven't a fucking clue."

Jack ran a hand through his hair and blew out a long sigh. Bed's gonna have to wait. He walked to the bar, pushing several unopened moving boxes out of his path, and poured three fingers of bourbon into the nearest glass. Stumbling back to the sofa, he set his drink on the second-hand IKEA coffee table and knelt to gather the weathered canvas case and the report.

The trip was a waste of both his time, and the Center's resources. Not because it wasn't important, but because no one knew what the hell to do about it. The doctors and nurses on the ground had everything covered. "Everything" consisted of keeping the patients comfortable and the IV's flowing. Without a clear cause, everything was considered. The uranium mines in nearby Krasnogorsk were ruled out as an environmental cause because no one there suffered from the malady. One by one, the researchers eliminated infections, poisons, viruses, biotoxins, and pretty much everything else they could think of. Regardless, twenty-five percent of the residents of Kalachi—most of them children—were suffering from a severe case of "you're fucked".

Sleep wasn't going to come easy tonight, even with the jet-lag. Jack reached for the remote and turned on the television, hoping late-night infomercials would do the trick. Instead, he was greeted with a breaking news report. He took a long sip of his drink, then listened to another disaster in the making as he turned the wedding band on his finger.

"Once again," the bottled-blonde newsreader said with forced gravitas, "the Germanwings Flight 9525 crashed 62 miles north-west of Nice in the French Alps in an apparent act of suicide by the co-pilot."

"Great. We not only have to worry about the planes and terrorists, but now the even damn pilots are trying to kill us." He surfed the channels, hoping to find something a little cheerier to watch, finally landing on an X-Files marathon.

***

The morning light streaming through the window was so bright it buzzed, vibrating his brain like the inside of an angry beehive. Jack sat up, holding his head as the buzzing grew more insistent. The gauze clouding his mind cleared enough for him to locate the source of the noise. He grabbed the cell phone from his briefcase, bumping his head on the coffee table and spilling the remainder of his drink. "Son of a bitch!" he said. The liquid soaked into the carpet, spreading like an infection, and he watched it grow before turning away and answering the phone.

"Morning, Mason," he said, rubbing his temples.

"Morning, buddy," Mason said, unnaturally buoyant for so early in the day. "How come you didn't call me for a ride from the airport when you got in?"

"It was pretty late. I didn't want to put you out."

"Of course," he said, "what else could it be?"

"Don't start, Mason," Jack said. The comforting friend routine was getting stale. It would be so much easier if everyone just let him be.

"Okay, okay," he said. Jack imagined the man holding his hands in front of him for protection. "I was just calling to see if you were coming in today. You know... to work?"

"What time is it?"

"Quarter to one."

"Shit!" Jack jumped from his seat, barking his shin on the coffee table that was now apparently trying to kill him. "God-damn it."

Mason laughed. "Don't sweat it, Jack," he said. "Sally said to take your time. She knows the trip was hard on you." Not as hard as Sally was when she was in a mood. Nominally his superior, his position was fluid enough she often had to ask rather than order. When she did order, though, it wasn't pretty. At all.

Jack looked down at the pictures, holding the phone to his ear with one hand and scrubbing his head with the other. "You have no idea, Mace."

"Well, anyway... Sally said to take the rest of the week off and come in fresh on Monday."

"Wow," Jack deadpanned. "A whole two days off. I'm honored."

"You're forgetting today is Wednesday."

"No, I'm not. But since it's past noon, today's already gone anyway." "That's the spirit!" Mason laughed again. "How about we meet up for drinks after I get off work, and you can tell me about your trip?"

"I don't think—"

"Not taking no for an answer, buddy." His tone softened, and he said, "Seriously, Jack, you need to do something besides work. Start living again."

Jack looked around his apartment at the bare walls and the unpacked moving boxes, both mostly untouched since the day he signed the lease almost a year ago. "Sure, Mace. I'll see you at Jimmy's around six. You get to pick up the first round."

"Deal."

Maybe it's time, Jack thought as he hung up, walking to the largest stack of boxes. The one on top stared up at him like the children he spent so much time with the last five weeks, forlorn and lifeless. The label on the side read "photographs." He frowned, picked it up in trembling hands, and placed it in the corner of the room closest to the door.

That one would be last. It had to be. *I'm not ready*, he thought. He wondered if he ever would be.

***

Jimmy's was a noisy place on the slowest of days, but Wednesdays were unique. The back room was devoted to an especially boisterous version of Trivial Pursuit that included teams, cheerleaders, and betting. The front was a frenetic mix of pool, parties, and piano. Most nights the musician was female, young, and pretty; tonight, however, a rotund man with long hair and a graying beard pounded the keys into submission. There was an abandon to his playing, fat fingers hitting more keys than intended at times, offering a simple elegance to his delivery. When Jack first walked in, he was greeted with a discordant—and in his opinion, more beautiful—rendition of Leonard Cohen's "Hallelujah". The man's voice was both grating and powerful, and choked when he came to the lines:

> *And it's not a cry that you hear at night*
> *It's not somebody who's seen the light*
> *It's a cold and it's a broken Hallelujah*

"I hate that song," Mason said as he slapped Jack on the back and sat next to him at the bar. "Same thing over and over again. Never goes anywhere."

Jack turned, shook his head. "I think that's the point," he said. "It's about the futility of life."

"Whoa," Mason said, popping a handful of peanuts in his mouth. "A bit early in the evening to go all philosophical and morose, don't you think?" Jack winced as Mason spoke, watching the man's hand dive into the bowl of complimentary nuts. Jack never ate those. Working in the field for the CDC's Global Health Center taught him the dangers of communal food sources; and besides, they were liberally doused with hot sauce in order to get the patrons to buy more drinks. In Mason's case it worked like a charm.

"If you'd seen what I had..." Jack began.

"Yeah, I read the preliminary report you filed," Mason said, shaking his head. "Sounded rough." He brightened a bit, and said, "On the up side, Sally took your advice and is sending in a second team and some serious equipment."

"Won't help," Jack said, lifting his beer to take a drink. He stared at nothing while he drank, imagining the pure, dreamless sleep those people endured.

What did it feel like? he wondered. *How is that any different than death itself?*

"But you said—"

"I know what I said. What I'm saying now is that it won't help."

Mason watched him for a second. "Jesus, Jack. Talk about morose." He waved at the bartender for a beer, then handed the woman his credit card to run a tab. He grabbed the bottle by the neck, took a swig, and said, "Let's get a booth so we can scope the ladies without looking like creepers." As he rose from the stool, he pointed at the nearest empty table. "That one looks good." He winked at Jack and waved his hand. "Full view of the room." Mason lead the way a few steps, then turned back. "And no more talking about work," he scolded, wagging a finger in Jack's face. "I get enough of that at work."

"Deal," Jack said, and followed him to the table, grabbing a menu from the bar on his way. "I don't know about you, but I could go for some wings."

"More of a leg-man, myself," Mason said, laughing at his own joke. Jack noticed Mason did that a lot, and had for as long as he had known him, going all the way back to college. Mason was tall and thin, but his presence filled a room like no one else Jack knew. Loud to the point of almost being bellicose, he had a knack for making any gathering more fun. He was the perfect counterpoint to Jack's staid seriousness. Especially lately.

Mason surveyed the room while Jack checked the menu. Both actions were pointless. The bar was lousy with regulars, and Mason had already hit on most of the attractive women—and been shot down—over time. Jack knew the menu by heart, and could write it out longhand if required. *At least with my nose buried in the menu, I don't have to listen to endless questions about my mental health.*

Mason stopped pretending to look at women and turned his attention back to Jack. "So... how are you doing? Really."

"No," Jack said, waving his hand in front of Mason's face.

"No, what?"

"No, as in 'we're not doing this now', no." He had grown impatient with everyone trying to help him. *There was nothing anyone could do to help.*

"Jack, it's been a year—"

"Ten months, twelve days, and two hours." Jack's eyes narrowed and he took in a slow breath. "I know exactly how long it's been, Mason. I don't need anyone to remind me." He rubbed the back of his neck, feeling for the scar. "I have an empty apartment reminding me every goddamn waking moment of my life!"

"Calm down, man," Mason said, his voice soothing. He reached across the table and placed a hand on Jack's shoulder. "I'm just trying to help. That's all."

"I get it, Mace. You're trying to help, Sally's trying to help, Jenna and Bill are trying to help. The whole goddamn world is trying to help, but the only person who can help me is me." He finished by pounding his fist once on the table, rattling his bottle. It danced to the point of tipping, but he snagged it with a deft swipe of his hand before it fell. A few of the regulars turned their way, but the rest ignored them. *Everyone's wrapped up in their own shit*, Jack thought. *They don't need mine, too.*

Mason pulled away, and leaned back. "Fine, I get it," he said. "Not another word tonight." He crossed his heart with the bottle still in his hand. "I promise."

Jack watched him with one eyebrow cocked, then sighed and took a long drink. "So..." he said, pointing with the neck of his bottle, "how about that one over there?"

Mason turned to where the bottle pointed, squinted, then shrugged. "Nah.

She turned me down last week."

"Woman's got good taste, then." Jack tried on a smile to see if it fit. Tight, but not uncomfortable.

Mason clinked bottles with Jack and grinned. "Damn straight."

***

With a long weekend to fill, Jack considered driving the two hours to Greenville where his brother Bill and his wife Jenna had the perfect life with their two children. As a police detective, Bill had a certain amount of flexibility in his schedule, and was certain to make time for a visit, but Jack knew the questions and concerns were sure to come up. Last night with Mason was almost more than he could bear, and an entire weekend of sad, sincere faces would drive him to drink.

He swirled the glass in his hand. *Okay*, he thought, *drink* more. He grabbed the remote and turned on the TV, then reached for the stack of mail he retrieved from the hold bin at the post office. Large enough to choke an elephant, most of it was junk. And bills. Always bills. The medical bills were the worst, most arriving months after he thought everything had been paid. The first one of those had a balance high enough to make him laugh out loud. "Might as well just ask for eighty bazillion dollars," he said. "It would be just as likely to get paid." He touched the long scar on his left arm that was the object of that particular bill. "Would have been cheaper just to take it off."

There were twelve more just like the first, all from different doctors and specialties—five were names he didn't recognize. Odds were they had just been standing near his door and had spoken to the real doctors once, giving them an excuse to sign his chart and try to take a slice. As far as he was concerned, used car salesmen were more honest.

Another late notice from the landlord, but since he already put a check in the mail, he threw that one away. The letter from Mark and Betsy he set aside unopened. Like the photographs in the corner, he would get to it later. In the middle of the pile was a letter postmarked from Kazakhstan dated two days before he arrived in that country. Odd, he thought. There was no return address, and he couldn't imagine anyone there who knew he was coming. The envelope had come open at some point during transit, and was resealed with tape. If he were a prominent figure in the government he might take it directly to the FBI for a once-over and let them open it, but he was neither that important nor that paranoid. Jack ripped the letter open at the end, extended his arm, and shook the contents onto the coffee table.

A standard A4, coarse-grained sheet of paper, folded twice, fell out and fluttered down. Jack held the open end up to his eyes, but there was nothing else inside. He set the envelope aside and carefully opened the letter, flattening it on the table. Handwritten cursive letters, formed by a thick soft-leaded pencil, lay there accusing him in English—*I know who killed your wife and daughter.*

"So do I, asshole," he said, grabbing his drink and downing the remainder in a single gulp. "I did."

***

"It's not working, daddy," Riley said, kicking the back of his seat.

"Sorry sweetheart. It's probably just locked up." He turned his head just enough to see her pouting in her car seat, "Do you know how to reboot it?"

"She's four, Jack," Beth said beside him, shaking her head, "not one of your tech geeks at work."

"Hey, the kid knows more than I did at her age," he protested, accompanied by the sound of Riley pounding on the tablet's screen.

Beth turned all the way around in her seat, and said, "We'll be at nana and pawpaw's soon, baby. You can wait a few minutes."

"Too long!" More pounding.

"Ugh, fine," his wife said, unbuckling her seatbelt. "I'll come back there and see if I can fix it."

"Just have her hand it to you."

"It's strapped to the back of your seat, remember," she said with a heavy sigh. Crawling between the front seats, one knee on the center console, her ass was beside Jack's head. He remembered that perfect ass was the first thing he saw the day he met her, and, truth be told, the first thing about her he fell in love with.

He smiled and reached across with his left hand to slap it, but never finished the motion. The truck, a big red four-wheeler with the knobby tires high school boys in Georgia loved so much, slammed into his side of the car. Not his door, of course. That would have been a blessing. No, it hit Riley's door full-on, folding the car nearly in half before rolling it over. Coming to rest in the ditch upside-down, the horn stuck blaring a single soulless note, Jack winced in pain as he turned toward his wife. Her lifeless eyes stared straight at him, marking him like a witness in a murder trial.

Riley wasn't even crying. Such a good girl. Brave, like her mother. Millimeter by agonizing millimeter, he continued turning—contorting his body to see behind to his daughter. His beautiful, perfect little girl. A foot, attached to an ankle, attached to a leg, attached to...

He woke screaming, sweat flowing from every pore in his body. Flailing his arms and legs, the dream releasing him reluctantly, he swept the three empty liquor bottles off the table next to the sofa. They fell to the carpeted floor with a trio of thuds.

Jack sat up, the screams replaced by sobs, and he hugged his knees to his chest while pulling his hair with one fist. He rocked in his seat and cried for several minutes. It was comforting in its way—familiar as an old pair of shoes. "It wasn't my fault. It wasn't my fault."

A mantra as old as his pain, he would repeat the refrain until he almost believed it.

"The asshole ran a stop sign. Happens every day. It wasn't my fault. It wasn't..."

What would his friends and family say if they saw him like this? Would they worry more, or be impressed by his ability to hold it together as well as he had? *What the fuck does it matter, anyway?*

Everyone told him it would get better. It didn't. It only grew more distant. The pain of loss did not lessen, it did not get easier. It was there in an instant, hammering on the door to his brain whenever he remembered his daughter. Remembered her...

"At least the son of a bitch had the decency to die," he said, his voice stronger now that he was fully awake.

Cops said he was asleep when he hit us. He sleeps forever now. Good goddamn riddance.

Jack picked up his cell to check the time. 3 am. He set it back on the table, and the phantom letter grabbed his attention again. He lifted it, turned it over, then back, looking for anything that might hold a clue as to who wrote it. *What's the point, anyway? Everyone knows who killed my family.*

"Mark Wilson Peters, Jr.," he said aloud, the sound of his voice mocking him. "He had help, though."

He threw the letter to the table, then stood on shaking legs. The pins in his left leg were hurting, and he rubbed it while he walked to the bar. Almost empty, it still held enough to keep him numb at least through Saturday. Sunday he would set aside for recovery before returning to work on Monday.

Until then he belonged to Jack Daniels.

SOUR

SOKW STALKED HER FATHER THROUGH THE FROST-COVERED undergrowth as he hunted for signs of the white-tailed deer. She knew he pretended not to hear her; the ground crunched softly under her moccasins, but both her deformity and the worn cornhusk doll she refused to part with betrayed her. It was the left foot more than the doll. A twisted thing, and while walking on it caused her much pain and embarrassment, she endured both as the daughter of Kitchi Machk should. The tribe's greatest hunter, he wore the skin taken from the black bear as a cloak. An only child, Sokw endured much from the tribe in her desire to be worthy of his love, never complaining.

Other than the foot, she was a pretty girl at eleven summers. Her hair, straight and black, was tied back neatly with a leather thong, and her face clean and open. Tall, like Father, she was slim like her mother, but Wawetsek had far more curve of hip and breast than she.

One day, she thought wistfully.

Mother was the most beautiful woman in the valley, and Father told Sokw that many suitors from every nearby tribe and clan competed for Mother's attention. Of all the men, only he had killed a bear with just strength and knife.

Sokw stumbled over a fallen branch, disturbing the silence of the late autumn forest. Father never admonished his clumsy daughter—she would do that on her own.

"Don't worry Chepi," he said. "I don't think we will find a white-tail today." Father called her Chepi whenever they were alone. It meant fairy spirit, and she knew that's how he saw her. Mother, though, named her sour when she first saw the deformed foot. Sokw would never be as beautiful as Mother, and would never command suitors the way she had.

"A little longer?" Sokw pleaded.

"No, Chepi," he said, walking back to her. "I think you've had enough for today." He swept her up in his great arms to carry her back to the village.

"I can walk, Father," she said with a dramatic sigh.

"The sweat on your brow betrays you, little one." He wiped her forehead with his free hand. "You don't have to always be brave, Chepi. Besides," he said with a great wide grin, "I like carrying you. There will come a time when you will not allow it." He hugged her tight. "I wish you could stay this age forever."

She wanted to protest, but it felt so good to be off her feet. Smiling, she nestled her head against his neck, comforted by the gentle sway of his gait.

"Just be sure to put me down before we reach the village."

A faint fluttering behind her head told her the pukwudgie were near. She lifted her head and looked back at the glowing little person following them. Father ignored the pixie, but they appeared to her with increasing regularity over the last year—watching from a considerate distance.

Always watching.

***

Wawetseka deftly skinned the last of the rabbits with her stone knife, cleaning each before cutting them up and placing them in the clay pot. Sokw watched in fascination. She could never follow her motions accurately, and Wawetseka refused to slow down for her daughter, claiming it was her responsibility to learn.

"Why do the little people follow me, Mother?" She kept her eyes on Mother's hands and knife as she spoke.

Wawetseka rolled her eyes and sighed. "It's been said they sometimes follow the feeble and slow-witted for sport or amusement."

Sokw shook her head. "I haven't seen them laughing at me."

Mother stopped her motions and sighed again. "You wouldn't, Sokw. They do not reveal their emotions to children." Wawetseka finished the last of the rabbits and set her knife aside. She took Sokw's chin in her hand. "You would be wise to avoid them."

"Yes, mother," she said, pulling away. It was difficult to avoid them though. They followed her everywhere, and she felt them watching her even as she slept, invading her dreams and leading her south into places she should not go alone. Father said there were worse things than bears or wolves in the south. That was where the Yakwawiak lived, and those giants ate children by the handful. He always smiled when he said that though.

Still, the pukwudgie were trying to tell her *something*, and she felt it was her fault she couldn't hear them. Days later, she woke to find the blood between her legs. The air around her sleeping mat glowed with the combined light of dozens of little people, and her head was filled with voices. *Blood*, grandmother once told her, carried strong magic, and the blood of *womanhood* held the greatest of all.

The gathering of pukwudgie spoke of great danger not only to the south, but all around. *North*, they said. *You must move your people north.*

***

Sokw tried for days to get someone to listen to her, but even Father thought it crazy.

"Chepi," Father spoke slowly, as if speaking to a small child, "the pukwudgie do not speak to the People." He shook his head. "Not ever." His face softened. "Your mother is a medicine woman, and has never heard them speak. Why would they speak only to you?"

It must have something to do with the blood, she thought, *but why did no other woman hear them?* She wondered if she might become a great medicine woman like her mother. *Maybe greater!* She shook her head, and thought, *Such pride is shameful.*

Father took the motion as assent. "Don't worry, Chepi, I'm sure it is just because of your change. Strange things happen to girls who are becoming women."

Sokw nodded. Some of her friends were acting strangely these days. Many of them followed the young Braves like dogs begging for scraps, shirking their in favor of braiding flowers into their hair. None followed Ahanu though. The mischievous boy was still too young. He didn't seem interested in girls, anyway. With a shock Sokw realized her friend might be two-spirit, and she smiled. *Maybe he will grow into a great medicine man. We might walk the same path.*

"Father, the little people *do* speak to me," she said at last. "They insist we move the village north, and something terrible will happen if we don't."

He shook his head. "This is the wrong time to move north, little one, and is dangerous all by itself. We should instead follow the river south." Father's tone left no doubt the discussion was ended.

***

"They won't *listen*, Ahanu." Sokw spent days trying to get even one Elder to hear her, but Mother always seemed to get there first, poisoning the waters. *It's her time*, her mother told them. *She is not thinking clearly.*

She and Ahanu were alone on the ground in the warm longhouse cutting strips of leather to weave into a bracelet. He always came to her with such projects, though she never knew where he found the materials. He did not hunt, and his own father died three winters ago.

"Maybe you can get," he pointed with his chin at the hovering pukwudgie, "your little friends to help you."

"I have asked, but they keep repeating time is growing short."

"Well... that's not very helpful," he said with a frown.

"Worse, Father says we will move south soon. Mother told Megedagik she sees a big winter storm coming." The Sachem always listened to Mother whenever the talk turned to the weather. It wasn't just that she was always right though. Sokw was sure the man was in love with her. Father never showed he took notice, but the talk around cookfires among the women was fierce and often unkind.

"Maybe we *should* move south, then," Ahanu said as he stopped his work and laid his hands in his lap. "Your mother is never wrong, you know."

Sokw stopped as well, a bitter response on her tongue, and then saw the twinkle in the boy's eye. She threw the leather at him, yelling You! and pounced. They wrestled in the dirt, laughing for a time, until Sokw gained the upper hand and pinned him to the ground beneath her. "Take it back," she squealed in triumph as she held him down.

"Sokw!" Father's head appeared in the longhouse's opening, one hand pushing the hide aside. "What do you think you're doing?" There was a strange look on his face that frightened her.

"Nothing, Father," she said, her voice catching. She and Ahanu scrambled to their feet, looking to one another for help. "We were just cutting leather for bracelets." Ahanu nodded vigorously.

"Come with me, Sokw," Father said, his eyes never leaving the boy. "We have hunting to do." He turned and walked away without looking back.

Sokw looked over at Ahanu, smiled weakly, and shrugged. She cleared her throat and said, "I'll help you later," then followed in the big man's footsteps. Outside, he handed her a knife, but no bow. He took up his own bow and a quiver of arrows and threw them over his shoulder to lie atop his bearskin cloak. He picked up a smaller fur covering and threw it at her, almost knocking her over.

"Here, it will be cold in the forest, and colder still by the time we return."

At first she followed down the hill in sullen obedience, trying hard to keep up with the brutal pace he set. Within an hour, she was limping, but he did not slow and she did not complain. They were heading east from the village into a part of the forest she did not recognize. If they did not stop soon, she knew they would come to Seepow Mahecaniittuck—the great river.

"Are we hunting the white-tail again?"

"Quiet, Sokw!" he hissed. "Try not to make so much noise when you walk." Father kept his eyes on the forest floor, looking for signs of his prey's passing.

"Are you angry with me?" she whispered. He stopped walking, and his shoulders slumped under the heavy bearskin. She stopped with him, the only sounds coming from the soft breeze rustling in the branches above, and the soft roar from the unseen river ahead.

Father turned to her and sighed. "No, Chepi, I am not angry with you." He looked around, almost *through* her, and then knelt, stretching his arms gently grasping her by the shoulders. "You are growing up, and it frightens me." He frowned. "And your visions frighten me even more."

She shook her head. "They are not visions, Father. The little people speak of *their* visions."

"Chepi... they don't—"

"Then why do they gather, so?" she said as she pointed overhead. Just beneath the lowest branches, pukwudgie by the dozens hovered above her like a glowing cloud.

Father sighed again. "Your mother said—"

"Mother," she sneered. "What does *she* know about little people?"

"Take care, Sokw," he said, wagging a finger at her. "Your mother is a great medicine woman of the tribe. She has earned your respect."

"She is not so great she hears the pukwudgie."

"Sokw!" A white-tail burst through the undergrowth, an arrow stuck firmly in its haunch. It stumbled past, knocking Father into Sokw, and they both fell to the ground. The deer, a young buck, bounded away,as Father turned toward the river. He scrambled to his feet, grabbed his bow and drew an arrow from the quiver. "Get back to the village!"

"I don't—"

"Go! That arrow was *Iroquois*." She knew he expected something, but she didn't understand his agitation. "One of their hunters is near," he snapped.

Sokw's eyes flew open wide. Her people sometimes traded with the Iroquois, but *never* meeting without a hunter or warrior. This side of the Seepow Mahecaniittuck was for her people, the other was theirs, but neither respected boundaries when gathering for winter.

Father rushed ahead without waiting to see if Sokw heeded his words. If the hunter was coming this way, and Father didn't stop him, it wouldn't matter what she did. With a last look back, Sokw ran toward the village as fast as her twisted foot allowed.

Running without care for silence, she listened to a great struggle behind. A war cry followed by grunting and the sound of underbrush crushed beneath heavy bodies. Overhead was the rapid beat of many small wings. The little people—so *many* of them—flew about her as she ran.

Inevitably, she stumbled. Her deformed foot caught on an exposed root, and she tumbled head–first to the ground. When her head struck the large stone, her last thought was *Of* course *there's a rock.*

***

Sokw drifted, soothing voices floating around her.
Will it live?
The blood has stopped for now. It may yet.
The Gathering is ready.
Now *she* was floating. *No,* she thought. *Swaying.*
Carefully, she opened her eyes. The forest was all darkness around her, with a harsh light above casting stark shadows on the floor below. *I'm in a tree!*
Yes, the voices said as one, *we thought it best. There are many bad things down there.*

Sokw nodded, but Father was also down there. *Somewhere.*

The bear that walks as a man left here after the light hid behind the trees.

"He's alive!" she squealed and clapped her hands, nearly toppling out of the crook of the tree. She sat up, but a wave of nausea struck her, and she lay down again. The ankle with the ruined foot throbbed, and she dared a peek at the purple bruising. Wind rustled the leaves as the branches swayed, and she shivered against the cold. Her cloak was gone. *Somewhere down there*, she thought, her head hanging over open air.

We can get it for you if you wish.

"Yes, please," she said to the light. There were so many of them they formed a great glowing ball as large as a wigwam. A dozen or more broke away from the main body and flashed into the forest, returning a few moments later carrying the cloak between them. "Thank you," she said, reaching for the fur. Pulling it tightly around her, she waited for her body to thaw.

Allow us, please. Several of them flitted underneath the cloak between it and her body. Soon the cloak warmed, heated by their eldritch glow.

She snuggled under the cloak and wondered what to do next. Climbing down would be very difficult with an injured ankle, but then what? She couldn't walk on it. Even if she used a branch for a crutch, the terrain was rough and treacherous enough in the dark with *two* working feet. Waiting for someone to find her was not an option, either. She might freeze to death before then.

The Gathering will carry you.

"You can?"

A tinkling of unmistakable laughter from the cloud. *How do you think you were brought here?*

"But it is such a long way," she said, her brow furrowing. "You can carry me that far?"

It is not far.

"But..."

We will open a Way.

"I don't understand," she said with a shake of her head.

The ball of light cycled rapidly from blue to white, laughing at her again. *We will open a Way.*

Dozens of the little people separated from the glowing mass above her, and flew a short distance beyond the branches in front of her, chasing one another in a large circle. Larger than the village's communal fire-ring, the pukwudgie within flew faster than her eye could follow. Brighter and brighter the ring grew, while inside that brilliance was a darkness blacker than a raven's feathers. No light penetrated that circle of flame—it was a hole in the air, empty of everything that made the world. Curiosity overcame fear, and she leaned forward to peer through—then she looked to the forest floor so far below, and the fear returned.

"Why is it so high up? Why not closer to the ground?"

Your village is on a hill. Passing through here at the ground would place you there underneath. That would not be good for you.

"Can you bring it closer? I cannot jump that far on one foot."

The Way is made as it is. It is as it will be. We will carry you across and through.

The rest of the Gathering flew to her, each grabbed a patch of the cloak in their hands to pull it away from her, stretching it as a rug on a floor. They lowered it a little, inviting her to climb aboard. Sokw reached out with her hand

and pressed the surface as a test. The cloak, held so tight, did not yield. It felt like a thick straw mat for sleeping.

You must hurry. The Way cannot hold. It will close soon.

She hesitated briefly, then climbed onto the cloak. As the little people adjusted to her weight, they flew toward the Way. Within the ring, individual pukwudgie flashed brilliantly, then disappeared.

"What is happening to them?" she asked, afraid of the answer.

They must give themselves to the Way. Their life feeds it. Soon, none will be left to hold it open.

"They are *killing* themselves to get me home?" It appalled her. She never asked them to sacrifice themselves for her; she was not worthy. It was too much, the burden too great, and she sobbed for their loss.

Head in her hands, eyes squeezed tight against the tears, she neither saw nor felt her passing through the Way.

***

The air above the village fire-ring popped, and a large circle darker than night appeared a few handspans above the ground. There were many people outside gathered by Kitchi Machk readying a search for Sokw, but instead saw her appear through the hole in the air, floating on a cloak carried by a host of little people. Father stared open-mouthed at her with wide eyes, but Mother watched her appearance with a calmly raised eyebrow. The rest of the village backed away in a stumbling mob, some wailing an making protection symbols in the air with their hands, while elders stood their ground.

Mother was first to Sokw's side when the pukwudgie settled her to the ground and held her as she cried. No one else in the village moved or spoke. Looking up, Sokw realized they were waiting for *her* to say something.

What she did, instead, was collapse into unconsciousness.

***

"Everything is being packed up, Sokw." Ahanu sat on the ground beside her sleeping mat where she sat, eating soup from a small clay bowl, her favored old cornhusk doll in her lap. "You were out for a whole day while they bound your ankle—it's not broken, by the way, just twisted—and then the elders met and decided."

"So they believe me?"

Ahanu waved at the hundreds of pukwudgie flitting around the longhouse and laughed. "What do you think?"

She frowned, remembering what it cost the little people. "I think we need to hurry." Sokw sat up a little straighter, scooting back to lean against a wall. "The little people spoke a lot while I was asleep, Ahanu." She bit her lip. "We only have a day or two."

"You have told no one *why*, though. That makes it hard for even the council to get people moving, you know."

She shook her head. "I know, but I didn't understand until now." Placing the bowl on the floor, she reached out and placed a hand on Ahanu's shoulder. "Everything here, and south for two days travel, will be gone." He opened his mouth to speak, but she placed a quelling finger on his lips. "Someone, somewhere, will open a Way like what brought me here... only *much* bigger. Structures larger than Yakwawiak, reaching hundreds or thousands of handspans high, will come here from the spirit world and crush this place beneath them." She watched his eyes widened. "Even the surrounding hills will be flattened." Drawing her hand back, she rubbed her head where she had struck the stone. It still hurt, but was at least properly bandaged. She felt strong enough to stand if her ankle would allow it.

"I know what you're thinking, Sokw, but you shouldn't leave the longhouse right now."

She searched his face and recoiled at what she found. Fear. He was afraid for her. "What is wrong, Ahanu?"

He looked down and picked at the edge of her sleeping mat. Finally, he looked up again and said, "There are many in the village who fear you, Sokw." His expression grew pained, and then angry. "Some are calling you a *witch*."

Sokw drew in a sharp breath. She knew there were some who would fear the display of the pukwudgie, but she thought no one would think her capable of witchcraft. She picked up the doll, pieces of it falling to the floor, and held it tight against her chest. Her voice shaking, she asked, "Who says such a thing?"

Ahanu looked down again, still picking at the sleeping mat, and would not look up. "Your father."

***

"He does not call you witch, Sokw," Mother said with more patience than Sokw thought she had. "But he does believe you to be possessed by the little people. He says we should not trust you to lead us from danger because there is none." Mother patted her hand, and the doll rattled dryly. "He thinks they lead us *to* danger."

"Why would the little people do that, Mother?" The pukwudgie fluttered about, shocked into an unusual silence. Sokw shook her head, "They have never shown themselves to be our enemies before."

"But they do play tricks, little one," Mother said. "And they don't always have a care for the danger."

Sokw nodded. She remembered the time they tricked Ahanu into pulling a beehive from a tree for honey. At least, he *claimed* they tricked him. No one saw what happened, only the aftermath with the many stings it forced Mother to doctor. It *was* a funny trick—even if he did almost die.

"Do *you* think I am possessed?" she asked, wide-eyed.

"No, Sokw," Mother intoned, shaking her head. "What I saw was a miracle, not a trick or the work of evil spirits." Wawetseka smiled down at her daughter, pulled the doll from Sokw's grasp and set it aside, and took both of the child's hands in hers. "For the first time since your birth, I am proud to call you my daughter."

Sokw knew she should rejoice, but found she could not smile.

"Do not worry, little one. Your father will soon see with clear eyes."

***

But Father did not see. He spent all of his time trying to spread his fear to the elders while everyone gathered for the move. The pukwudgie became increasingly frantic, their numbers swelling beyond counting, each whispering warnings to Sokw. She tried to plug her ears to block them out, but they spoke directly in her head, and even in sleep they filled her dreams with their words and images.

They showed her great structures—like longhouses stood on end—each large enough to house entire villages, stretching to the sky. So many they blotted out the sun. Each was made of stone, with patches of something like ice at regular intervals. The little people called the ice *windows*, and said they would never melt even in the hottest summer. Most of the—*buildings*, they called them—fairly sparkled in the sunlight. Some were completely covered in windows. And all the while their words conveyed *soon*—until this morning, when they spoke in unison.

Today.

Sokw woke with a start, the voices gone, but the feeling remained. *We must move now*, she thought, and began by grabbing her pack. Remembering how the pukwudgie created their Way, the size of this one caused her to shiver at the thought of how many souls it would take to open it.

More than all the People from the River to the Sea, she thought.

She checked one last time to be sure she had everything and noticed her doll was missing. It was with her when she walked around the village yesterday, but she was sure she brought it back.

Pulling the hide covering aside, she stepped out of the longhouse into a village in complete disarray. Most families were loading the last of their belongings onto the sleds pulled by both men and the dogs they used as pack animals. They had already transported the food stores north to a temporary camp. Today the rest of the village would move as one to their new home, taking everything. The little people were clear—*nothing* would remain of the village after today.

"Ahanu," she waved to the boy as he tossed his belongings onto a sled. Men on either side were busy positioning and tying things down.

"Finally awake, I see," the boy said with a grin. "These people," he jerked a thumb at the growing crowd, "honor you far too much. They let you sleep while there is work to do."

"I have never known you to be a friend of hard work, Ahanu," she said, smiling back. He snorted and took her pack to place it on the sled beside his own. "Have you seen Mother and Father?"

"Wawetseka is with the other medicine women, gathering supplies I think. I have not seen your father."

Sokw shuffled her feet for while she looked down, then leaned in to whisper, "Have you seen my doll?"

A snicker escaped before he controlled it. "No, Sokw. If it is not in your hands, I do not know where it is." He peered into her eyes long enough for her to become uncomfortable. "Isn't it about time you set that ratty old thing aside?"

She didn't know what to say to that. Instead, she looked past him to the crowd of villagers beyond. She hadn't spoken to Father once in the past few days, and she bit her lip as she searched for his face.

"I need to speak to Megedagik. The Sachem should know we must leave now."

"I knew it was today," Ahanu said. "But are we really leaving now?"

Sokw nodded. "The little people insist. *Now* is the only word they say." She left him there and walked as fast as her foot would allow in search of the Sachem. *Maybe he will get Father to see*, she thought.

***

The village moved at the Sachem's command, every household with their packs, sleds, and families leaving their wigwams and longhouses behind. It was still early, and there was snow on the ground, but everyone walked with purpose. Some in the village felt the same as Father, but they would never question Megedagik.

She had yet to speak with, or even see, Father that morning. There weren't so many in the village she should not have run into him at least once; and now, traveling as one, he should have been easy to spot. Even in a tribe of great warriors, Kitchi Machk stood above them all.

Mother walked beside her, a place of honor at the front of the procession with the Sachem, a pained expression on her face. Always under control, Mother usually maintained

122

a mask of perfect calm. Today, though, the mask was cracked and broken. The beauty was still there, but lines of worry marred its perfection.

"Mother... is something wrong?" Sokw feared the answer. The little people knew something, but lapsed into silence once the trek began.

Wawetseka did not look at her daughter. "Kitchi Machk follows his own path, Sokw." She shook her head, and a tear tracked slowly down her cheek. "He will not be with us at the camp."

"Where..." but she already knew the answer. He refused to believe. He remained at the village. The village that would soon disappear. "*No*," she cried, and turned to run back to find him. Megedagik grabbed her as she tried to pass him, sweeping her up in his arms and throwing her over his shoulder like a felled fawn. She screamed and clawed at his back, imploring him to release her, but he ignored her until she relented. Still he carried her, tossing her at last to the ground when they reached the new camp well after mid-day.

***

Pukwudgie flitted about her, the word *no* projected into her mind over and over. Sokw did her best to ignore them, but the intensity behind that single word brought more pain than hours of walking on her twisted foot.

"Please, Ahanu, I need your help." Her eyes moist and red, she knew her friend would not refuse her, but the fear of discovery remained.

"You will die if you go back, Sokw," he said with a shake of his head. "Besides, you are being watched. I don't think you can leave the camp without someone seeing."

She leaned closer. "That's where *you* come in."

Her plan was simple. Ahanu would do what he always did—be a nuisance, but big enough to gather all eyes to him while she slipped away. She knew he would agree since he couldn't help himself when it came to causing chaos. He settled for tossing a large bundle of smudge sticks onto the communal fire, and in the resulting noise, smell, and confusion, Sokw sneaked away. Ahanu was to keep her presence alive by telling anyone who asked that he had just spoken to her.

Sokw ran, pukwudgie fluttering about her head, heedless of the pain in her foot. She could not move fast with the ground covered in a light dusting of snow, but she hoped she had enough of a head start that none would catch her before she reached the village. What she would say to Father when she got there, she did not know. She only knew she had to *try*.

The ruts from the sleds ran true, but she also knew there were places where she could cut through the trees to avoid the turns they had taken. She did not know how much time was left, but she was sure to make it back quicker than the journey out.

The smoke from the village fire rose from the top of the hill. The clearing around the village was large, so she was still a great distance from Father as he stood at the perimeter watching her approach. He was smiling and holding her doll to his chest as he would a small child. Stroking the cornsilk hair, he seemed to be singing to it. Sokw stopped, watching him, the gentleness of his touch a memory on her skin. She wept to see the greatest of warriors felled so.

"Father!" she cried, and he looked up with hope in his eyes. She started forward, but the pukwudgie gathered between them, refusing passage forward.

No, they said. *It is time.*

"Quickly, then," she said aloud, "bring him to me!"
We cannot. Behold.

Light brighter than the sun blasted beyond the village to the south, and the very air shattered. A wave of force flattened the surrounding brush and trees, knocking them both to the ground and scattering the pukwudgie like so many leaves on the wind. When the wave passed, there was the *city* gleaming just beyond the village. Father was facing away, then turned to her with wide eyes and a huge smile on his face.

Now he knows, she thought. *He sees!*

One of the closest buildings, one side sheered off by the edge of the Way, broke apart and began its slow rumbling tumble to the ground. Many of the buildings did the same in either direction around that outer edge, and Father spun again.

"Father, run!"

Too late, Chepi, the little people said.

Father knew it too. He turned back to her with a smile, and waved goodbye as the building collapsed in a great cloud of dust and rubble, covering the village, and burying him beneath.

***

The tribe built a stone cairn where Kitchi Machk fell, draping a ceremonial bearskin over a pole erected there. Once the dust settled, braves scouted the territory, and finding the buildings empty, Megedagik allowed the tribe to move into those around a large wooded area near the center.

"I think he saw me, at the end," Sokw said as she sat, shucking an ear of corn with her new knife. It was a brightly polished silver-colored metal, thinner and stronger than the copper knives braves used to carry. They found many such things in the city, only a few they understood.

"No," Mother said as she worked beside her. "He saw a medicine woman."

"Maybe, but..." Every time she thought of Father now, it was only the things she missed about him. Never what he meant to her. He was her protector, not just from the world, but Mother. Now everything was different, and while she no longer needed his protection, she missed it still.

"Death is a part of life, Chepi," her mother said with a wan smile. "The Great Spirit decides for each." She patted her growing belly. "And when life comes as well."

Sokw sighed and smiled back at her mother. Setting aside her knife, she turned to the pile of corn husks. Selecting several, she began fashioning a doll for her sister.

In a world where Europeans never colonized the Americas, a young Mahican girl finds a powerful talisman in Central Park in the middle of modern-day New York City.

This began its life as a short story (separate from the previous Sour) and I realized early on the concept was just too big to stay within those lines.

SWIFT THE RIVER FLOWS

CHAPTER 1

SÍIPUW, AWAKE BEFORE DAWN, SAT ON HER SLEEPING MAT, her dark eyes wide and alert, watching the first harvest yellow and orange rays of sunlight peek through the heavy weave covering the doorway. A riot of mottled light and dark like fairies dancing with the wind played over her oval face, warming her smile, and she leapt from the mat, her long hair trailing like black flame. Still dressed in yesterday's clothing, she stuffed her small feet into her best pair of hiking moccasins, grabbed the pack from the flat top of the oak stump at the foot of her mat, and hurried toward the door. She paused only long enough to take a leather thong from the pack and tie her hair back, stuffing the long ponytail into her shirt. Raven-glossed and unadorned with feathers or flowers, it was short work keeping it neat.

"Free day!" Síipuw whispered as loud as she dared to her cornhusk doll atop the wooden shelf over her bed; she had only this season stopped carrying it wherever she went. Wmíisan allowed her apprentice one day per moon as a well-deserved break from chores and studies, and always the day after the full moon. Her people were Wolf Clan, so "one

127

day to howl," as Wmíisan told her with a toothy grin, "was not too much." The old medicine woman expected Síipuw to spend the time with her friends—*Hmph*, she thought, *as if there* were *any*—but she would use this day as she always did... *exploring*. She pulled the door covering aside and stepped into the glow of morning sun. Wind rushed past, flinging dust and leaves from the clearing into her room, tossing sheets of writing leaves and marking sticks to the floor. Clear jars of medicinal herbs and roots reflected splinters of light around the tiny room like a spell gone wild, and she smiled before dropping the cloth. *I must clean and straighten up before dusk*, she thought. Wmíisan had a habit of inspecting the room after a free day; the woman expected work even when none was required.

Her room was part of the old woman's wigwam and had its own opening to the clearing. Most mornings, Wmíisan sat at the fire ring outside their doors, her tight, sour face watching Síipuw's doorway as the young girl dragged herself out. On free days, the old woman either slept in, or was already in the village proper selling her services.

The snoring from the woman's doorway, a hungry bear growling deep inside its cave, told Síipuw she was sleeping in. Her heart swelled at the thought of not having to explain her plans for the day. Lying to Wmíisan was impossible, even if was something Síipuw could do—which she could not. She had never told a convincing lie in her life and had given up trying long ago. *Always best to be honest, or say nothing at all*, she thought. Her pack—filled last night with jerky, dried fruit, rope, and other necessities—hung from one shoulder. As she passed the fire ring, she took two clear containers of water hanging from the pole of hooks, paused, frowning, and grabbed a belt and knife. *You can never be too careful*, she remembered her father saying. It was one of the last things he had said to her. He lived on the far northern end of the Wood, but had not come for a visit since the day he gave her to Wmíisan as an apprentice.

That had been two harvests ago.

I won't think about that, she frowned, then forced a smile. *Today is for the Wood!*

A sharp intake of air from Wmíisan's wigwam, told Síipuw she tarried too long. She turned from the fire ring and fled in silence across the clearing toward the hard black path separating the Wood from the strange and wonderful buildings beyond, most so tall they touched the sky.

***

Síipuw didn't *plan* to visit the forbidden place when she set out this morning, but here she was, looking up and up at the odd stone man aback a prancing stone horse. A man unlike any she had seen before, he was dressed in Builder's clothing, hair shorn short, with a tuft of coarse hair covering his upper lip. Two others walked at his side, both looking like the People of her village. There were strange symbols at the base of the marker, much like everywhere in the Builder City surrounding the Wood. Even in the Wood, there were smaller stone buildings with the same writing. Wmíisan told her Old John understood the marks, but Síipuw didn't believe that possible. He lived far from the Wood, taking residence in one of the holy places filled with the writings of the Builders. To Síipuw, he was more legend than real.

Behind the Stone Horse, steps led to the huge doors and unknown dangers—or treasures—within. None had entered—or so she'd been told—since the buildings first appeared. *Someone must have, though, or the place would not be forbidden.* Few of the other buildings were, and her people had explored them all.

129

She took a step forward, and a light flashed from her right, arrowing toward her. The pukwudgie flitted in front of her face, his life-light spinning through a series of colors, the sweet scent of honeysuckle in his wake. Síipuw knew he meant to stop her; the little people had kept a close watch on her ever since she became an apprentice. She wondered many times if Wmíisan had asked them to, though the woman had shown no ability to speak with them. Síipuw recognized this one, the right pair of iridescent dragon-fly wings smaller than the left, a single nick on the larger pair marking her little friend as clearly as if his name were painted on his tiny gray chest.

"It's okay, Wãhs'nanégan," she brushed the pukwud-gie aside with a wave, "there is nothing to fear here." *I hope.* She had given him the name *Bright* more as a com-ment on his life-light than his intelligence. She frequent-ly wondered if that was fair. She took another sliding step, and Wãhs'nanégan returned, round black eyes blinking, hands waving frantically; he hovered at the end of her nose, his loincloth of squirrel hide flapping as he shifted to stay in front of her. He carried a short spear tipped with haw-thorn in one hand, and he grinned like a cat as he jabbed the point into her flesh.

"Ow!" she cried, slapping at the little pest, but he was too swift. She felt her nose and wiped a tiny drop of blood from the end. "Ugh," she said in disgust, then pulled the pack from her shoulder. "Fine, we'll do this the hard way." She fished inside, removing a tightly wrapped cloth package. She untied the string and unfolded the cloth to reveal hard bread and a small container of honey. Pinching off a piece no larger than her thumb, she spread a drop of honey on the bread, then set it on the ground beside her. The pukwudgie brightened at the sight, his color now a glaring white, and dove to the ground to feast.

"That should hold you for a while." Still rubbing her nose, she lifted the pack to her shoulder and sauntered away from Wãhs'nanégan as he dug into his treat. She passed near the Stone Horse, an urge to touch the base gripping her, but she kept her hands reverently to her side. She looked up the steps, straightened her back, and climbed. The sun was still low in the sky, and light poured inside, casting long and angular shadows.

She stopped at the opening, a pulsating *wrongness* pressed against her, holding her a step away. The protection spell she cast on her clothing last night—one of the first Wmíisan taught her—glowed from the gentle assault of the building, and she breathed deep before stepping across the threshold.

Inside, the dank air prickled her skin. She sniffed, lifting her nose and flaring her nostrils. The air in this one held a third quality she could not identify. The closest she could come was *age*. That was silly, though. *All* the buildings were older than her grandmother's grandmother.

Her eyes adjusted to the gloom in stages, the light from outside reaching only as far as the entry. She looked up into the darkness ahead, and her eyes grew wide as breath caught in her throat.

Dragons!

In the center of the largest enclosed space she had ever seen were the bones of two dragons frozen in mortal combat. Wmíisan had told her about such things, but never having seen one, Síipuw hadn't believed. Her breath and heart quickened as she shuffled forward. Her protection spell glowed brighter as she neared the beasts, casting its own wan light. The urge to touch them was strong, but even as the glow warded, it also *warned.* The magic of this place was more than she knew, and far more than she could handle.

"Don't touch, then," she said, her soft voice echoing around and around. "Understood." She dropped a hand she hadn't realized was already reaching. With much regret she left the two behemoths behind, each screaming a silent cry in their dance of death, and she continued her search through the forbidden place.

***

By the time her stomach complained to be filled, Síipuw no longer felt the wary tingle at the back of her neck the way she had when entering. It was still there, but muted through constant pressure. The glow of her protection spell had faded, but she did not know if that was because of a lessening danger, or because the spell was failing. Either way, she did not wish to spend the night there.

She had seen much since she entered the gigantic structure—most of it odd and unknown to her—but it was clear it was the place where the Builders brought things they valued so others could stand in their presence and share a history. It was the same with people everywhere in her experience, with their paintings, craftwork, and totems. The Builders were no different.

Síipuw sat on a flat stone in front of another animal—this one looking almost alive—surrounded by desert grass in a clear cage. It seemed to stalk a smaller creature, both frozen in time. Neither was familiar to her. She took the pack from her shoulder and set it beside her on the stone, then removed a package tied in string like the one with the bread. The jerky inside was deer, the last of what she traded for the last time she had gone to the village. Next to it was a small amount of dried fish she had caught and smoked.

She bit off a large piece of the jerky and chewed, listening to the sounds of the building. Mostly silent, there were still things to hear for those patient enough to listen. A distant squeak and squeal of mice. The wind hooting and howling through empty halls. A steady drip of water falling from a great height to splash on the stone floor. Amid all this, a clear and near-silent hum like the voice of a single small child.

Ghosts of children—*otschitschachquan*—inhabiting empty places was not unknown to her, but this did not sound like that. This was the sound of a living thing. Síipuw stood, shoving all but the jerky into her pack. She slung the pack over her shoulder and felt the knife in the belt at her hip. The cold metal was more comfort than her spell, and she wrapped her hand around the hilt for reassurance. She took another bite of the jerky before searching for the sound.

She passed one open room after another, knowing what she hunted was not in any of them. In one, light spilled in from a break in the clear panels mounted high on one wall. In another, water dripped from a tree branch that had broken through the roof. A small pool had formed in the center, the water green and brackish, and the smell drove her onward before she could linger.

One doorway led to a set of stone steps, the clear tone coming from below, so she started down. By the time she reached the bottom, the only light was from above and the dull illumination of her protection spell, so she took a glow wand from her pack, bent it in the middle until she heard a snap, and shook it. The wand glowed much brighter than her spell, and she held the thing in front of her with one hand and fed herself the rest of the jerky with the other.

Glow wands had been a recent find of her people, and like most things in this world, had taken them a while to discover their function. One building held what seemed an endless supply, and in many colors, but her clan kept the location secret. Like every other discovery, the number was finite, and they could make no more. It galled her that most of her clan used them only for ceremony; they wasted many of the Builders' gifts in this manner.

Opposite the stone steps, a doorway opened into another large chamber, and across that expanse was another hall. The sound, though not louder, was clearer now, and she followed it without thinking. Her protection spell warned her of no danger, but she was wary regardless. The air was thicker here, a blanket of green moss covering her face. The odors were like honeysuckle and spoiled fruit. Her footfalls, loud and clumsy, echoed from every surface.

Síipuw stopped before the opening to the hallway, listening. Damp, stale air pulsed in and out, breathing like a large bear in winter slumber. The sound neither wavered nor strengthened. It was still at the edge of her hearing and had been so since she first heard it. This was a magic with which she was not familiar, but unlike most of the building, it did not feel wrong. Síipuw stepped across the threshold, and her protection spell snapped off like blowing out a candle.

She should have been afraid. *Should* have returned to the light of day. What a girl of thirteen seasons *should* do, and what she actually *did* were often two different things, and Síipuw was no exception. She forged ahead, trusting her blade to protect her, and she drew it from the belt. She shuffled forward down the long hallway and stopped at an open room. Here again a broken pane of a window scattered the sun's rays, filtered between the branches of an overhanging tree, and filling the room with shafts of soft and shifting light. She entered, holding both the wand and her knife before her as proof against any living thing inside.

In the center of the room were several altars with clear cages on top, each holding items she recognized. Ceremonial bowls of clay or hammered copper, obsidian blades, and even pipes for smoking. Along the far wall were more of the cages and shelving, each holding similar items. None of them interesting. She could have held items just like them in Wmíisan's home. Síipuw shook her head and turned to leave, but before she took a single step, the sound changed in pitch.

She turned back to the altars, one drawing her attention. The clear pane on top had shattered, but nothing inside was missing. A collection of stone knives were laid side by side, and the arrangement suggested it was still complete. All but one was smooth except for the chipping necessary to fashion the blade, but the larger one in the center had designs carved into it she almost recognized. *This is the source*, she thought, passing a hand over the knife. *It sings.*

"What good is a stone knife?" she mused, her lip curled in a soft sneer, as she held out her knife of shiny metal the Builders provided. The stone knife, though larger than the others in the case, was still smaller than the blade in her hands. It looked to be ceremonial, as if intended for ritual sacrifice.

And yet...

And yet she felt no evil from it. Items used for ceremony always took on the nature of their use. A knife used for evil *was stained with* evil.

This one clearly was not. *Manitou* was present in everything, living or not, and once a thing's soul touched darkness, no amount of scrubbing could clean it.

The soul of this knife, as clean as anything she had known in her short life, called to her. It *begged* to be held, taken from this dark place, and she reached for it before she realized what she was doing.

Everything costs, she thought. *Scales must be balanced.*

With less reluctance than she thought she would feel, Síipuw lifted the stone knife from its honored resting place, leaving her metal one behind as payment.

The singing stopped.

***

A gale-force silence surrounding her like a cocoon, Síipuw half-stumbled toward the opening to the darkened hall as if her memory had been hollowed like a dugout canoe. She tried to remember the sound, but found she could not, and discovered she already missed it.

When she stepped into the hall, her protection spell emerged as if it had never left, asserting itself in a glow that drove back the dark. The heavy stone in her hand must have had an old spell, and a powerful one at that. Light bleeding from the edge was warm and bright, outshining both protection spell and the glow wand. The ruddy illumination from the knife lanced ahead of her, throwing every stone, turn, and opening into stark relief.

Síipuw paused, frowning and tilting her head at the combined light from the two spells. She took almost too long to realize the truth of what they told her. There was danger here, and for the light to be so strong, the danger was both real and close. She spun in place, listening for anything unusual while peering into the darkness past the reach of her light. *Everything here is unusual*, she thought as a shiver crawled up her back.

She heard it before she saw it. The soft pad of large paws, the hot breath of a predator stalking its prey. The low and throaty growl told her it was close, but nothing stepped from the shadows.

"You are reckless!" Wmíisan had told her often during her training, and she had been. *Still am*, Síipuw thought. Her protection spell was only good against evil magic, not a flesh and blood creature intent on killing. For that you needed a weapon. A spear or bow was best, but a good knife would do.

But she had left her *good* knife on the altar. All she had was the warm stone in her hand.

What good is a stone knife? she thought for the second time that morning. Why had she not brought a spear? Or even a bow and quiver? She had never been good with the bow, but any fool could use a spear.

The *thing* stepped into her circle of light from a near-by room, and she almost ran at the sight. Running from a predator was always a mistake, even when you had a place to run. In this space there was nowhere she could reach for protection before being run down; choosing to remain still saved her.

The animal was a large cat-like beast, malnourished and mangy, its thin coat of white fur dirty and scabrous in places. It prowled just outside the brightest circle of her light, never crossing its boundary. The eyes of the cat were rheumy, weeping white fluid at the corners, and it had a thick fluff of pale tawny fur surrounding its head. As skinny as it was, it still outweighed her by another two Síipuws, its paws each as large as her head.

She had never seen such a creature before, though others told tales of huge cats hunting in packs farther north where larger prey thrived. A Sachem in the region wore one of the skins as his raiment of office. They knew the animal as a fierce hunter, and like any wild animal, hunger made them more dangerous.

"You don't want me, mister cat," she said, her voice tiny and mouse-like to her ears. "Even with only a stone knife in my hand, I will make you work too hard for your meal."

That was all the bravery she could muster; just keeping her bowels and bladder from letting go was an effort. The animal continued to prowl outside the circle of light. Gathering all her courage, Síipuw slid a step forward, the light moving with her.

The cat shrank from the light.

Síipuw almost smiled, checking herself at the last instant. Showing teeth to a predator was an invitation to fight. Even children still on the teat knew this.

She slowed her breathing and took another step forward, and the cat moved to stay outside the circle. Another step, then another... and soon she stood at the bottom of the steps that had brought her here. The cat was between her and the steps, and if her next did not make it move out of the way, she had no other ideas. It had stopped circling, content to stand between her and escape. She had no wish to force the thing to back its way up the steps ahead of her. A single faltering step would be her doom.

Her stomach growled, and for a brief instant she feared the noise would encourage the animal to pounce. Instead, it tilted its head like the puppies in the village. Síipuw grinned—*without* showing her teeth—carefully dug inside her pack and pulled out the package of fish. She waved it in front of the animal, spreading the scent, and when she had its attention, tossed the pack of food behind her and away from the steps.

The cat leapt past her, so close it could have swiped at her with a single paw, ripping through clothing and flesh on its way. Instead, it landed on the free and easy meal, tearing the cloth off to gobble down the meager offering.

The way now clear, Síipuw breathed a heavy sigh of relief, wiped the sweat from her brow, and climbed the steps. The cat would follow her when he finished his meal, but if the light from the two spells held, she would see daylight again.

She turned to bid the cat farewell, but it and the food were gone.

***

Síipuw shaded her eyes with one hand as she stepped through the main doorway and into the blinding light of day. She cast a longing glance back inside, vowing to return with the next full moon. Ahead, the trees across the path still rustled their song in the breeze, the grass beneath still green, the sky above still blue, but the world without seemed *lesser* now. Behind, she felt the pull of dark magic, taloned arms reaching from inky depths to drag her back, but she felt no fear. Magic was a tool. A knife to cut, or a needle to sew. It only became evil when *used* for evil.

Why is this place forbidden? she wondered. *Other than the possibility of becoming a big cat's next meal, of course*, she thought with a chuckle. She shook her head, smiling, and walked down the front steps and past the Stone Horse, and this time she *did* touch it, feeling the coarse stone and smooth metal. Outside in the strong noonday sun, her protection spell was invisible—as was the spell surrounding the stone blade—but she could feel their presence. *Especially* the blade. It had its own flavor, reminding her of the smell of the first flare of burning tobacco.

139

After the tension in the hallway, her *own* smell was certainly distinctive, the pits of her arms soaking the shirt through. There were places where she could wash before returning to her home, but it might be best to leave it for now. She didn't know what to make of the knife just yet, and she didn't want Wmíisan to know about it until she did. Síipuw hoped the spell on her clothes masked its manitou, but washing them clean would break the protection spell.

Water cleanses everything, Wmíisan taught her. *Much strong magic begins and ends with water.*

She might wash the knife, but if that broke the spell—not a sure thing—would it also break the magic of the blade? And there *was* magic in the blade, Síipuw was sure of that. Objects containing magic were rare and required great power and skill to make. Some were made by Mother Earth in the fires of her belly, and others by Gitchi Manitou as he strode across the sky. The most dangerous were those made by men and were unpredictable and often overpowered. *Manitou* was a part of everything, but some things could hold much more before they burst. A shaman might die finding that limit.

Wãhs'nanégan flitted from a branch across the way, hovering in front of her face, the nostrils of his wide nose flaring, scolding her with a wagging finger. He had waited for her, possibly for a second helping of bread and honey. She sensed nervous energy from the pukwudgie, and she smiled lopsidedly to calm the poor thing. Her grandmother told her she had an ancestor who understood the creatures' speech, but Síipuw never had, nor had anyone else she knew. When he refused to calm and move away, she gently brushed him aside and continued toward the Wood.

Síipuw drank from one of her water containers, only now recognizing her thirst. The air inside the Place of the Stone Horse had been so water-heavy she had never thought to drink. The water was cool as it traveled down her throat, and she wiped her mouth dry and sealed the container, smiling at the sun. It was mid-day, and still no one ventured to this part of the Wood. None of the children she knew were brave enough to pass so close.

A small white-tail deer stood at the edge of the Wood, munching a sapling, and staring warily up at her with one eye.

"No worries, little one," Síipuw said with a wink, her voice soft and soothing, "I hunt no meat today." She paused, remembering the hallway. "Keep an eye out for the big cat, little deer. You would make a good meal for him, I think."

The deer, mollified, continued its meal, pulling the stem with a sharp tug from the ground before lifting its head to chew. It watched Síipuw enter the Wood, tracking her with its head pivoting on its long neck. Satisfied there was no danger, it bent back to the foliage.

***

"Where have you been?"

Wmíisan stood at the entrance to Síipuw's room, arms crossed over her slender frame, her right foot tapping the hard soil.

"Out," Síipuw said with a casual shrug. "Today was a free day, right?" She stopped farther away from the woman than manners required—almost at the fire ring, afraid to come closer for fear the old medicine woman might smell the magic of the stone knife.

"Of course, of course. I only hoped you might have brought back a root or two. Maybe berries for our meal."

Síipuw hung her head in real shame. Coming home empty handed was not only rude, it was selfish. She had taken food and water with her and brought nothing back. Well, not *nothing*, exactly, but nothing of value to the home.

"I apologize." She lifted her chin a tick. "Should I go find something?"

Wmíisan wrinkled her nose. "No, I think you should clean yourself. Your smell is frightening the rats." The old woman laughed loud and hard at her own joke, wiping a tear from her eye. She did this at least once a day at Síipuw's expense, whether alone or in a group. It was never nasty or mean, the way some children were, but Síipuw gritted her teeth and bit back a response. She knew the old woman was keeping the young apprentice in her place.

"I think you are right," she said, holding back the rest. She took a bucket from the post where it hung and started for the well.

"The clothes, too, while you're at it," the woman called out. "I fear they will reek come morning time. Probably contaminate the whole wigwam," she added, chuckling.

Síipuw knew her smell wasn't *that* bad, but it was best to placate the old woman. Wmíisan kept a stripped sapling handy for those times Síipuw forgot. The woman had not struck her in many moons, but that didn't mean she wouldn't.

She had to go to her room for fresh clothes and passed Wmíisan along the way. The woman stopped laughing and snatched Síipuw's arm, holding it in an eagle's grip with her bony fingers.

"Hand it over." As calm as the morning sea, she held out her other hand, palm up..

Síipuw thought to feign confusion, but there was no point.

"Come, girl, I can smell the magic in it. It must be very strong, or your protection spell would have hidden its scent."

Síipuw was a head taller than the old medicine woman, having shot up like a stalk of corn this season, but command was not about height, or weight, or how loud you could yell. It was about *respect*—how much you had, and how much you gave. Wmíisan had Síipuw's, no matter how much she wished it weren't so.

She pulled the knife from her pack and dropped it into the medicine woman's hand.

As soon as it touched her skin, Wmíisan let it slide away and fall to the ground. She stepped back, eyes wide, holding her shaking hand over the thing, first and last fingers out in a defensive gesture.

She looked up at Síipuw. "Where did you get this?" she asked, breathing hard and hunched over like her belly was sour.

"I..."

"Where did you get this, girl? Tell me!"

"The Place of the Stone Horse," she said, eyes lowered in shame and fear. "I wanted to see inside, and—"

"*Inside?*" Wmíisan shouted, and she released Síipuw's arm as the other hand flew to her mouth. She took another step back. "You can't! *No one* goes inside, Síipuw. It is not possible!"

Síipuw. Not "little one". Not "girl". Not "clumsy oaf". That, more than anything, shook her. The knife was *not* evil—it couldn't be—but the medicine woman acted as if it were. *What have I done?*

"Quickly, girl," the woman was saying, "wrap it in cloth, the heaviest you can find. Soak the cloth in water first." Wmíisan had calmed somewhat, but her hands still shook. "After you have done that, bring it inside," she said, then turned on her heels and staggered into her wigwam.

Síipuw stared after her, then shook herself and followed Wmíisan's instructions.

What good is a stone knife?

EXPIRATION DATE

EVERBODYS GOT UN, YA KNOW. I WOKE ONE MORNIN LAST year bout harvest time with that expirey date in ma hed, cleer as bells. November twelve, two thowsan sixteen. Most peeple dont know thers, travlin through the day as purty as ya please, blind to the world. I aint never been blind, though. Even when I dint know ma date.

Its a freein kinda thing, that expirey date. When ya know yur leavin this world on a certain day, it kinda means ya aint got ta care bout yer ownself so much. Take yestidy noon—I knew that car werent gonna kill me, so there werent no danger pushin the girl out the street. People sez Im slow, but Im plenty fast when it counts, yessir. Lil Dolly Miller only gots a scraped knee, stead o a smushed head.

Dont get me wrong, I aint no man o steel. I can be hurt, an hurt bad. I jes cant be kilt, is all Im sayin. Leastways, not till ma expirey date.

Ol man Barker sez Im nuts, but he aint all there his ownself. I ketched him peekin in the Millers winder one time when Im out walkin the widder Austins dawg, Bitsy, an the ol man boxed ma ears real good fer pointin out that warnt his house. Miz Austins a good ol gal, but Bitsys better. That puppy is always hoppin ta see me when I step up to the fence, an she barks a storm at ol man Barker—leastways, she been doin that the last week or so. Dont know why, but thats a good un right there. Barkin at Barker. Ha.

Anyways, I wuz tellin yall bout the day I went an saved the world.

Wuz a Thusday, iffin I recalect correct-like. Most evenins me an Alice—thats ma fren from way back—is sittin on her porch swing, swayin and recalectin bout the ol days. She dont call me nuts like Barker duz, but thers a sad kinda look in her eyes when I talk bout that expirey date.

"Charlie," she sez, "nobody knows when theys a gonna die. That theres up ta the Lord."

Now Alice dont say it like that, them words an all (heck, I dont think shes even a believer) cause shes smart. Not like I use ta be, but that wuz a long time ago. I jes has a hard time memberin is all. I dont argue with her when she say stuff like that, cause it just makes her more sad like. Alice wuz ma girl fer a time back when I wuz smart, but we dont talk bout that no more. That makes her sad, too.

Wes both too dang ol anyways.

"Whutcha think I get us some tea ta sip on while we swing?" she sez.

"Sure," I sez back, "I cud go fer some tea." I smak ma lips, "Lots o ice. Its a mite hot tanight." It aint full night, yet, but the daytime sun dun gon an baked that heat right inta the groun like a oven. The science guys keep a babblin bout global warmin an stuff like that, but Ima thinkin its jes the sun a heatin up. Its as good a idee as any, but I can tell Alice dont think to kindly bout it. Jes like she dont think to much bout most o my idees, an I know she wishes it were like the ol days wen I wuz smart.

I kech her cryin bout it wen she thinks I aint lookin, but dont say nuthin. I usta cry bout it to, if I wer tellin the truth.

Ol Man Barker walks by an we both wave, and I nuj Alice a bit, pointin out the fact hes heddin over to the Millers agin. She giggles all girlie-like, even tho shes well past her sebemties like me.

Bitsy starts a yappin ta let me know Ol Man Barker is a passin by her propity. I gess I should say hes a mite younger n me—by at least a good twenty year—but thats whut the kids call him, so the name dun stuck. We won talk about whut theys a callin me. I dun boxed a few ears my ownself over that, so the meen kids mostly jes leave me lone. The gooduns I smile and wave and fun aroun with. I also save a few... like lil Dolly.

That pups stirred up sumpin powerful, tho, and I sits up ta take a looksee. Cross the street, thers a Barker-shaped shadow squeezed twixt Bitsys fence and the Millers house. I knowd heda been headin that way, and knowd he wuz a plannin to peek in agin. But hes at Dollys winder now, an that dont sit right with me. Nosir.

That swing slamd hard into the porch railin when I jumpt off an ran into Alices front yard. When I got to the gate I yell "Hey Mr. Barker," an that shadow froze up solid as a block o ice. Bitsys a tearin up n down that fenceline ta beat the ban, barkin the hole way. I open Alices gate, but the shadow skitters off behind the house, an beats feet away down the street. the screen door slams behind me, an I turn ta see Alice lookin at me funny-like an holdin two swetty glasses o ice-tea. I close the gate an walk back to the porch.

"Whut wuz that all bout," she sez, settin them glasses on the table by the swing.

"Jess a shadow. Bitsy wuz a barkin, so I got up ta see whuts whut." I shrug my sholders an climb the steps, "Twarnt nothin."

But it were sumpin, an I decided then an there ta keep my eye on Ol Man Barker.

***

Next day, Barker comes over to the lil ol-folks home where I spend my goldun years. Thats whut the peeple whut run the place calls em—Goldun Years, like you can hear them captal letters. I dont see nuthin gold bout gettin ol, but them peeple act like its better n slice meatlofe. Leastways I gets ta visit with Alice in the evenins, and thats alrite by me.

Anyways, the Ol Man comes in an asts fer me at the desk, an the ativties lady come an gets me rite in the midle o Jeopardy! Can ya imagin? It aint like I know the ansers no more, but its fun wachin the smart peeple mess up. I laugh reel hard at the gooduns. Barker pulls me out to the front lawn ta talk all privit-like, an I figger he aims ta pologize fer peekin in lil Dollys winder.

"I need yer hep, Charlie," he sez, an I step back a bit. He dun sprized me, thats fer sure. "But first," he sez, "I need yer word a onner that you aint gonna say word one."

Now I dont go round givin my word ta jes any ol body—specially a peeper—but I wuz also powerful curios. Part o me wants ta know reel bad bout whut hes gonna say, but the bigger part dont want no part, if ya get ma meanin. Them to parts restle a mite in ma hed fer a bit, neether one givin much groun, an the hole time I wuz standin ther like a dummy.

He sez, "Whut do ya say, Charlie?"

I looks up at him an sez, "I caint give no word lest ya tell me whut I wuz sposed ta keep ma trap shut about."

Barker looks me up an down a bit, then nods an sez, "Yer the only one can get me by the widders dog, and I needs ta see whuts goin on in the Millers hous."

I squint at him all meen-like an sez, "That wuz you last night, warnt it?" I aint big, but at my age dont nuthin scare me. Ol Man Barker steps back and his mouth turns down.

"Cmon by muh place tanite, an Ill show ya why ya need ta help me." He leens in reel close, an sez, "We gonna save the world, Charlie."

Now ma ears don prict up at that. Like I sez, I ain no man o steel, but I ben reedin them pitcher books a long time, an I sure wood like fer once ta be one o them guys. Mabey show Alice I wuz still good fer sumpin.

Cept maybe without the runnin aroun in ma underware part. That always seem dum ta me.

***

Sos I dont tell Alice nuthin that evenin bout my visit with Barker, but I wuz reel sad bout that. It aint like reel lyin, but close nuff. Momma use ta box ma ears bad when I lied, an I learnt that lessen rite quik, lemmee tell ya! Ther aint no point ta lyin leastways... jes means ya gots ta keep trak o yer stories. An like I sez, my memry aint so good. One memry I kep from wen I wuz smart wuz whut it felt like ta be lied to. I dint like that to much, an I can still tell when someuns doin it ta me.

I took ma leave bout nine, an walked ta Barkers place over by the ralerode traks. His propity buts rite up aginst the slope wher the hardscrable spils down, but his hous is set way back near the fenceline. It meens hes bout as far out as a nayber can be, an evrythin he does sez he likes it that way. Me, I think peeple shud be nayberly, but it aint my place ta say.

His long driveway is peegravel, an ma shoos make crunchin noises as I walk up the way. Its a calmin sound, an I shuv ma hans in ma pokets an whisle a mite as the

149

moon follows me all the way. Barkers a wavin at me from his front porch, tryin ta shoo me along, but Im old enuf that I dont hafta move no fastern I wanna. I figur if he got sumpin importent ta tell me, it can wate. Its the lies an piddly stuff that hasta be tole fast—like them lawer comershuls.

I mosey up ta his steps, an he sez, "Glad ya made it!" all excited-like. "I warnt shur you wood."

Hes a pullin me along up to the porch, an I sez, "Tole ya I wood, an I keep ma word."

"Yes, yes," he sez, leadin me inta the house. Thers a odd sweet smell that hits me rite in the face when we walk in the door, but I dont say nuthin bout it—that wood be rude. We dont stop fer the usual plesentries of him showin me his home, insted he jes keeps walkin to the back. "Im runnin outta time, ya see, an if I dont do ma job soon, well..." he sez, an spreds his hands out and shrugs like I wuz sposed ta know whut he means.

"Everbodies got ta do ther job, I gues," I sez. "I thot you wuz retired, tho."

"Nah," he sez, walkin faster. "I gots a sorta free-lans job. Here," he stops at the seller door and drags it open. Thers a odd kinda lite comin from the bottom o the steps, an he shoos me ahed.

I looks at him like hes crazy, an I sez, "I aint goin down ther. Leastways not till ya tell me whut fer."

He sies real big, an he sez, "Its prolly better if I show ya. You wont believe the tellin."

Imma thinkin hes rite, ther, but I dont sayso. I turns back to the lite, an look down. Like me, them steps wuz ol an rikity, an dint look none to safe. Still, I figur it aint too fur ta fall if I slip. I start down, an I feels him rite ther at ma back the hole dang way. I been nowin that ol man fer years, so I dont fear fer him pushin me down them steps, but if he fell, wed most likly both be kilt.

Well, him at least. Ma expirey dates still a few days off. I cud still get stove up purty bad, tho.

We get to the bottom, an I sees the place wher the strang lite wuz a comin from. Its a big ole ball, reel shiny-like, no biggern a man is tall. I can see myself like it wuz one o them funhouse mirrows, an I wave at the other me. Hes smilin back an wavin like he knows me. Barker calls it his ship, but I dont see no perpeller or even no sales, so I sez I dont figger how it can move roun on the water. He sez it aint that kind o ship. This ones fer flyin in space! I look hard, but dont see no wings, so I figger hes tryin ta fool me.

He sez "Do ya know whut a alein is?"

I think on that, an sez, "Ya meen like the boy whut mows the widders lawn?"

"Nah," he sez, "not ileagal alein." He rolls his eyes like ma uncle use ta, an sez all slow-like, "A space alein."

Now I wuz tremblin a mite, I aint to prowd ta say, an I sez, "the kine whut ate them peeple on the big space refinry in that movee?" That thing gave me the heebeejee-bees when I wached it on teevee, an I never did wach the others—tho Alice tole me the forth one o them wuz prety funny.

"Thers good kinds, an thers bad kinds," he sez. He thumps hisself in the chest an sez, "Im the good kind."

Im still lookin at that ball an shiverin bout the bad space aliens, but I aint worryed bout dyin. Thers a work-bench off to the side with all kinds a sciency stuff like that place I member wher thay useta do those spearamints wen I wuz yunger. On the pegboard over the bench are a buncha things that look like guns, only theys shiny like the big ball.

"I wuz sent here ta stop one o the bad aliens from destroyin the Erth, but Im runnin outta time," he sez, movin twixt me an the pegboard. "I dun trakd them bad ones to this here town, but I werent sure who they wuz until a cuple a days ago. Im pretty sure theys the Millers, an the wors one is that littleun, Dolly."

I snap to when I hears the lil girls name. "I think ya gots a screw loose, Bob." Oh, dint I menshun his full name? Bob Barker. Onlies it aint the guy from the teevee, nosir. That one likes dawgs. I laff ever time I think o his name.

"It aint funny," he sez. "That lil girl is a powerful bad alein, an I meen ta stop her peeple baffor they can blow up the world."

"I aint helpin you kill no lil girl, Bob," I sez, an then I laugh a bit cuz I jes caint help it.

"No, no," he sez real kwik–like, wavin his hands at me. "I need ta get close nuff to use that thing over there," he point to one o the guns on the wall, "to scan em. If theys the ones, Ill use that," he points to anuther, "to encapasitate em so I can take em back to ma world fer trile."

Now all that souns resonable, but I aint convinced, an I sez so.

"I can pay ya fer yer truble," he sez. He smiles reel big an nods, like hes a tryin to get me ta nod along with him.

"Nah," I sez, "Im good." An I am. Ever since Alice hepped me take them docters to court bout fitty years ago. I aint rollin in it, but I aint never had ta sweep floors agin.

"I can do other things, Charlie. I can take ya with me to ma peeple. Show ya a hole other world. If ya want, thay can even make ya smart."

Now I caint say ma ears dint prik up a bit at them words. He wuz promisen a lot, an had upt his offer rite kwik.

"Tell ya whut, Bob," I sez, smilin at my ownself, "Ill hep ya do the scan-thing, but thas as fer as I go."

"Thats all I need, Charlie," he sez smiling back, an he slaps me hard on the back. "We haffta be kwik, though, cuz I think theys plannin to blow up the world on November twelve."

So thats how my expirey date became *everbodys* expirey date.

***

Full dark cept fer the moon, we walked to the Millers, keepin to the shadows. Barker wuz carryin his two shiny guns in a odd bag with no zipers or nuthin. I wached him shuv the guns right thru the side like it warnt ther. He kep wisperin the hole way bout his world an how prety it wuz, the nice things his peeple gonna do fer me, an how hes been gon too long. I stop lisnen baffor we get out his driveway, but he keeps goin. Some peeple got ta keep talkin so they knows they still thinkin. Its whut ya hear wen they aint talkin that tells ya the most.

I cudnt get the kweschun out ma hed—Whys they blowin up the Erth? I meen, thats a fare kweschun rite ther, an I cudnt think a no ansers. Barker wuz to bizy talkin, so I cudnt get a word in edgeways.

He shut up wen we got close to the widders hous. Bitsy come runnin up ta meet me, an Barker hung back a mite wile I calm her down. She liks ma han, an I scrach behine her ears. That tales a waggin like a seelin fan, an she hops a few times, but she dont bark. Wen shes setteld, I waves Barker aroun, an he walks over to the side between the to houses. Together we shimmy twixt the hous an the fense, an then Barker hans me the bag wile he grabs a trashcan ta set unnerneeth Dollys winder. Thers still a glowin comin from inside, so I know shes up past her bedtime.

I sets the bag on the groun so I can help him clime up onta the can, an then I hold him stedy wile he reeches fer the sill. He pulls up on the sill an peeks thru the winder, an turns ta me an nods. I smile an nod back. He points down an nods. I points up an nod, but I dont unnerstan the game. He makes that face ma uncle useta, and sies real hevy. He points an wispers real loud, "Ma bag."

"Oh," I sez, an bend ta pic it up, but Bitsys alredy got hold of it thru the fense. She commenses ta pullin it thru, an I let go of Barker ta ressle Bitsy fer the bag. Bitsy digs rite in sense we plade this game bunches over the years. She starts ta growlin an shakin her hed from side ta side, an that gets me ta wobblin. Ol Man Barker yelps an comes a tumblin off the trashcan, fallin over the fense inta Bitsys yard.

She dint take to kindly ta that, and she let go the bag an starts a barkin to wake the ded. Barker is stove up, but not so much he caint take a swing at a lil dog, an thats jes whut he dun. Lites is comin on aroun the nayborhood, an then Bitsy grabs the bag out ma han and beats feet inta the hous thru her doggy door. By now everone within earshot is on the street, and the Millers have come round the side. Mr. Miller is a big man, an looks nuthin like Dolly. Fact is, he looks like a meener vershun o Jon Wane, an he takes Barker by one ankel and drags him back over the fense.

Alice come acros the street an asts whuts goin on. I dont know whut ta say, so I keep ma mouth shut.

"You want me ta call the cops?" she sez, lookin from me to Mr. Miller whos still holdin Barker up by his ankel.

"No," sez Dolly, peekin from aroun her mommas legs. "I think daddy wants ta have a talk with him first."

Everbody standin around thinks thats a grand idee, ceptin me. I dont say nuthin, tho.

That lil girl tells her daddy ta bring Barker inside, an asts me ta come to. I sez I think Id better go home, but she sez it won take long. I caint see no way ta say no with everbody standin ther wachin us, so I say okay.

I starts ta walkin, an I think, *Some days it dont pay ta try ta do no good deed.* Dollys smilin at me as she takes ma han.

***

Inside the Millers place—wich is reel nice, by the way—me an Dolly sits on the sofa with her mom a wachin, and her daddy drags Ol Man Barker to the back room ta chat. Leastways, thats whut the missus said thays doing, but I dont hear no chattin. Fact is, I dont hear nuthin thru that door.

Dolly looks at me an smiles that sweet lil smile, and pipes rite up an asts me whut I wuz doin with Barker. I dun tole ya I dont like ta lie, but I had a powerful need to rite then. I dint, tho.

I look down at ma hans, countin the rinkles an livr spots, an sez, "He sed you wuz a bad alein, an he wuz sent here ta take ya back ta his world for a trile." I look up inta her big green eyes, an I node rite then it warnt true. "I wuz sposed ta help him get by Bitsy so she woodnt bark, but insted I muckt it up reel good."

Dolly laffed, like bells ringin, an clapped her lil hands, "That ya did, Charlie." She looked over at her ma, who nodded back. "I prolly shud tell ya everthing," she sed.

An she commensed ta do jes that. She tole it slow—not like I wuz a chile or a ijit, but like she new how fast I

155

cud lisen. Turns out Barker is the bad alein, an he wuz sent here ta kill lil Dolly. Her ma an pa are not her ma an pa in reel life, but aktully her body gards. Shes some kinda ruler on her world. She had ta splain it werent a wood ruler like whut my ma wood pop ma nukels with. This kind is like Presdint Obama. She wuz hidin here from the bad aleins till shes growd up enuf ta sit on her throne, an she sed if he had kilt her here it wood a created some kinda innerstelar insident. Sed her peeple wooda jes come here an blowed the place ta smithereens.

I tole her I rekon I wuz glad I messed up then. She sed she thot I messed up cuz deep down I dint beleve Barkers story. Sed it had sumpin ta do with my subconshus. I dont know bout that, but shes powerful smart, so I say okay.

Her pa—who aint really her pa, I gess—comes back inta the room, an tells everone that the reel Ol Man Barker been ded fer bout two weeks. Thissun kilt him, stuffed him in a closet, an took his identy. I sed its reel lucky this one looked and talked like the orignal, cuz weda all node rite kwik otherwise. That lil dog had him figgered out from the get-go, tho. Aint the first time a lil animal bested me.

Dolly looks at me an sez, "Fer yer good deed, we have enuff room ta take ya back ta our world fer a visit if ya like."

I think on that, then sez, "Can Alice come with us?"

"If she wants," she sez. "Ther is enuf room fer both of you, but we most likely won be comin back." She britens a bit, an sez, "An if ya want, our docs can make ya smart. Heck, thay can even make ya yung agin."

***

I tole Alice everthing, but Dollys pa had ta hep her beleve it. She sed okay ta goin with me, an thats how my expirey date come true. Ma dreem sed I wuz leavin the world on November twelve, an sure nuff, thats whut we did. I got ta wach the Erth get small as we flew away in the shiney ball, and Alice stood beside me the hole time holdin ma hand. We both sed no to the gettin yunger part, not reely wantin to go thru all that agin. I also sed no to them makin me smart.

I wuz a ijit before I wuz smart, an a ijit after. I figur bein a ijit is easier—ya by yerself a hole new bach o problems when yer smart, an thays bigger ta boot. I figger now that bein happy meens septin whut ya are and whut ya have, insted o whut you want. Took me a long time ta unnerstan that, tho Alice dont jes yet.

Shell get ther.

A few years ago I joined a wonderful little critique group. We met once a month at a Denny's and offered advice on everyone's stories, going around the table for each. Sometimes the discussions were deep, sometimes raucus, and always fun and respectful. That's because Michael Gibson was our group leader, and one of the nicest guys you'd ever want to meet.

Last year he passed in his sleep, and the world lost one of the good ones. Huh? was one of his favorite comments about a story that didn't quite work, and this story is in honor of him. I think people who know him would recognize him straight off here.

HUH?

I SAT ALONE NURSING SCOTCH NUMBER THREE AND TRYING hard to ignore my reflection in the mirror. Wife number two had abandoned hope, packed her bags while I pounded the pavement looking for work, and took a cab to the airport for parts unknown. I drank the last of my unemployment, slammed the glass on the pitted bar, and motioned to the pretty little bartender for another. Blond ponytail swinging, she slid a frosty beer to her only other customer at the opposite end, rolled powder-blue eyes at me before snatching a bottle, and poured my cab fare into the glass.

"Last one," she warned, doe eyes turning up to mine, fake lashes batting.

"If you say so." I fisted the tumbler, and downed half in a stroke.

She eyed me for three seconds with a single raised eyebrow, then turned back to her duties. I was alone for a reason and we both knew it. I didn't have enough cash to get drunk, but *numb* was an attainable goal. The girl would kick me out soon enough, but without cab fare I was gonna sleep it off on a park bench.

Most people faced with a self-destructive half-drunk would have kept to themselves, sipping their nasty Heineken and leaving a man alone. Not Gibbs. What I know about the man now would fill a fair-sized encyclopedia, but *then*? All I knew then was he was more interested in running a bar con than self-preservation. As a regular, I had seen it before. He gave me that look they saved for the rubes, took another sip to show this was unplanned, then sidled over to the seat beside me.

"Evenin' friend," he said, eyes shining. Just like that— like we *were* friends. I got an itch in my skull that said we probably *would* be. I didn't like it.

I nodded and sipped, preparing for a hasty retreat as soon as I heard the "can't miss investment opportunity". It paced behind his eyes like a caged tiger. Or lion. Probably a Liger. The man was short and round with prominent ruddy cheeks, bulbous red nose, and a full mane and beard that was mostly white—a down-on-his-luck Santa Claus on a three-day bender. He had a large ring on his right hand that looked like stainless steel. The fedora he wore was new, as were the boots. He climbed into the chair and swiveled, leaned on the bar, and laughed as if perpetually on the edge of a smoker's hack.

"Troubles?" he asked.

I made a face and shrugged. "No more'n anyone else."

He furrowed his brow and eyed me like he was deciding which suit to wear. "Nah... look's like you could use a friend." He nodded at the change I had showered on the bar to pay for this drink. "Down on yer luck, too, I bet."

"Wife's got the checkbook," I said with a grin I didn't feel.

"I bet." He relaxed, took another swig of his beer, and set the bottle off to his right. "Hey... wanna see somethin' that'll make you go *huh?*"

As a first line in a bar con, it was mildly original, but the way he said it—tilting his head and scrunching his face like he'd tasted sour milk—had me nodding in spite of my mood. "Sure," I said, my curmudgeon's mask slipping.

"Watch this." Gibbs fumbled an ordinary coin from a vest pocket and placed it flat on the bar top. He grinned at me and winked, eyes twinkling, then waved his hand like a magician over the coin. The coin followed his act to the letter and lifted into the air six inches and hovered. I had seen this levitating trick once before, but he seemed to enjoy it more than me. Gibbs moved his hand first left, then right, and the coin followed like a hungry pup, remaining exactly six inches above the bar. After a few seconds of this, he slammed his hand down, pinning the coin beneath, a single bead of sweat forming on his temple.

"Ever seen anything like it?" He looked like a kid with a new chemistry set. I watched him turn his hand and expose the coin. He nodded, and I took the hint, picking it up.

"Once or twice." I turned it over in my fingers. It was a penny, though not your average copper.

"Noticed that, did ya?" He waggled his eyebrows at the coin. "Steel. The only way the trick works."

So... not a con. Just a nice guy trying to cheer a sadsack. I cocked an eyebrow at him and grunted, refusing to voice my revised opinion.

He pushed away from the bar and pointed to his thigh. "See? Got an electromagnet of my own design strapped to ma leg, its miniaturized twin in this ring." He fluttered the fingers of his right hand under my nose. "Flip the switch, and the magnetic gradient from the multiple poles holds the coin in place between the two. It even follows the ring when I move my hand." His smile, broad now, was wholly infectious, and the corners of my mouth turned up in sympathy.

It's not every day a man loses his wife and gains the world. I turned the coin over again, reading it twice to be sure. Me and Gibbs *were* gonna be great friends. A man should always be friends with a wizard—technological or otherwise. I thought of all the kids who might've turned away a young Bill Gates. Or a prepubescent Gandalf, for that matter.

"Got a problem there." I handed the coin back to him. "The date on that penny is 1974."

"So?"

"They made the *steel* pennies in '43." I pointed at the coin. "*That* one is aluminum." He looked lost for the first time that night. "Aluminum isn't magnetic."

He tilted his head, tasting the milk as two overhead bulbs popped and died.

"*Huh?*"

THE STONE OF TANTALUS

CHAPTER ONE

IF EVER THERE WAS A DAY FOR SKIPPING CLASS, THIS WAS it. The sky was blue without a cloud in sight, a faint chill in the air, and the pretty girls were out in force. Jason Callahan wasn't much for skipping, but that didn't mean he couldn't enjoy the walk across campus. April on the campus of the University of Texas meant the women's shorts were high, the t-shirts tight, and the blond pony tails swayed in rhythm when they walked. From his first day on campus, it seemed every girl was a perfect ten, and even now he still marveled at the sight. Jason smiled, shoved his hands in the front pockets of his faded jeans, and began the long walk across campus from Jester East to Moore Hall. He had at least an hour before his Quantum Three lecture, so he took his time, strolling with his usual lanky gate.

A tall and pretty redhead passed him going the other way, dipped her chin and smiled as she reached up to brush a spray of hair over her ear. He smiled back, *almost* turning, when his cell buzzed once in his back pocket.

Kat always knew. Jason might not stray, but he *was* an unredeemable flirt.

He stifled a laugh, then pulled the phone from his pocket to check the text message.

Lunch after class?

He poked large fingers at the screen, correcting several times, *Only if I don't have questions for the prof after,* then hit send.

Less than a minute later the phone buzzed again with the message, *As if.*

This time he did laugh.

Kat knew him better than he knew himself. She was always a step ahead of him in life, and he was grateful for it. There were times he grew complacent his first year, but when she joined him on campus in his second things shaped right up. *He* shaped up. It was the same throughout middle and high school. From the day they first met she was his personal drill sergeant, urging him to "get his shit together." Nothing she said or did ever felt as if she were nagging, though his friends laughed every time she pulled him into line.

Which is often.

The air was dry that morning, the early fog shooed away by a demanding sun, so he parked under a tree and watched other students hurry to their classes. Urgent and earnest freshmen were easy to spot, as were the sophomores convinced they knew everything. Seniors seldom made their presence known outside of class, grinding to finish what they started. *Juniors* were a different breed altogether. Members of the student body long enough to know the ropes, but still just *students* rather than soon-to-be-graduates.

Kat was only a sophomore, but she knew the best places to eat (Conan's), where the best music was on sixth street (a running debate), and when to avoid that area altogether (ROT Rally). An Army brat, she soon adjusted to each new environment, and was already an Austin native while he still felt like an outsider. Coming to Austin was, for him, like stepping on a new planet; every social gathering a First Contact situation fraught with diplomatic danger.

Keep Austin Weird! The shirt, worn by a shambling dreadlocked sophomore, yelled at him in all-caps as the boy passed. *The cannabis is strong with this one,* Jason thought with a smile. He had one of the t-shirts stuffed in a drawer in his dorm, too self-conscious to wear it. The damn thing felt like a statement on his own personality, rather than the odd-ball parts of the city.

"How long you gonna stand there watchin' the girls like a creeper?" Jason's roommate, Dan, slipped in beside him and leaned against the tree.

"Damn, dude. Never saw you comin'."

"Too busy scopin' trim," Dan said, smiling. "If I'd a been a snake, I'd a bit ya." He waggled his eyebrows as his mouth snapped.

Jason laughed. Dan wasn't as dense as the Central Texas twang led most people to believe. Jason was sure it was a deliberate act on Dan's part—like Jason learning Spanish without ever telling anyone. It made for a major advantage at times. Although with no one to practice on, he was forced to watch telenovelas on the Spanish language channels when no one was around.

"And I'm not girl watching," Jason protested.

"Hey, I won't tell Kat if you don't." Dan grinned again, "I don't want to have to clean the blood off the floor when she cuts yer nuts off."

"True that," Jason said, and lifted a fist to bump knuckles with his roommate.

"You comin' out to play some pool tonight?"

"Nah. Gotta work in the lab until nine." Other than his grants and scholarships, it was his only source of income. He worked hard to avoid the student loan trap that snared so many of his friends, but those programs only went so far. Work–study was a joke in many departments, but Physics seemed to get it. They worked him hard, but with enough pay and hours to make ends meet.

"Too bad," Dan said with mock sympathy. He raised an eyebrow and grinned. "Guess I'll have to entertain Kat for ya."

Jason laughed. "Yeah," he said, smirking. "You let me know how that works out for you."

Dan smiled, then checked the time on his cell. "Shit! I'm late for class. Again." He looked around at the bevy of young ladies, then to the sky like he was beseeching a deity. "Fuck it," he said. "Just Geology anyway." Everyone on campus called it *Rocks for Jocks*, and was famous as the only lab science you could pass without ever setting foot in a lecture. Dan set his backpack on the ground, fished around inside, then pulled out a beat up Frisbee. "Wanna toss it around a while?"

"Damn, Dan, that's some serious old–school shit, there," Jason said, shaking his head. He pulled his cell out of his pocket, checked the time. "I've got exactly twenty minutes."

***

"If you're that interested, Jason, you know Feynman's lectures are available on the internet." The lecture today didn't answer all his questions, and as usual, he spent the time on the way out drilling the professor for more.

"But what about situations arising from having two independent single spin waves? The energies you calculated on the board seemed a bit off. Here..." Jason took out a

166

pen and looked for something to write on, but Kat stepped away from the wall by the door and took his arm.

"Dr. Harrell probably wants to go to lunch, Jason," she said, steering him with a gentle nudge away from the harried man. "Just like *I* do," she finished with a smile. From the first day Jason met her, it was the smile that bridled him.

"Next week, then," he said to Dr. Harrell, allowing Kat to pull him away. She hooked an arm into his, handing over her book bag for him to carry.

She frowned, looking him over. "Don't you *ever* carry any books or paper to your classes?"

"Nah. I like to travel light."

"How do you take notes?"

He tapped the side of his head with a forefinger, "It's all up here, babe."

"You always took notes in high school," she said, squinting at him. "And don't call me babe."

"That was mostly for you. That and I hated all the other subjects in high school. It was all I could do just to stay awake in class." He smiled. "Here—especially this year—everything I'm taking is something I'm interested in." He leaned over and kissed her on the cheek. "You'll notice I have never taken notes about *you*, either."

She rested her head on his shoulder as they walked. "What day was our first kiss?"

"Uh..."

"Maybe you *should* take notes," she said, laughing.

Part of him wanted to complain that no one kept track of such things, but the rational part knew better than to voice it. That path only led to a full-blown argument rather than playful teasing. Most of his friends had been through several girlfriends in the time he had been with Kat, and they often asked him how—some meaning *why*—he stayed in one relationship so long. *It's all in knowing when to keep your mouth shut*, he thought. *Knowing when to pick your battles, and when to surrender.* Neither of which had anything to do with being right.

"So, where are you taking me for lunch?"

He looked down and smiled. "We could walk back to Jester," he said. "I've got plenty on my meal card. My treat."

"I've got a biology lab in an hour."

"Kismet Cafe, then?" he shrugged.

"Sure. I'll buy, though."

"Hey, I got this," he said, sniffing.

"You got any cash or a credit card on you?"

"Uh..."

"Like I said, Mr. Callahan. *I'll* buy today."

And that, apparently, was that. There was no arguing with her once she last-named him. Jason still bristled at the idea of her paying for so much—his upbringing so steeped in the male mystique—but it wasn't as if she didn't have the funds. She rode in her freshman year flush with scholarships and lots of cash from her parents. And even though she didn't *need* to work, she still put in a few hours every week tutoring local students for extra money. Money he knew would help *him* with his expenses.

Money was fungible, as the economics majors were fond of saying, so he couldn't get shake the idea the engagement ring with the tiny diamond he had hidden in his dresser was paid for with *her* money. *Ah, well*, he thought with an inward sigh, *at least if she says no, she gets her money back.*

"So serious," she said, snuggling close. "What are you thinking about?"

"I'm thinking if we don't hurry, you'll miss your lab and my stomach will eat itself."

She laughed as he picked up the pace, matching him stride for stride.

****

The Computational Physics lab was as quiet as a library. Most students wouldn't begin serious study for another couple of weeks. Tonight it was just the regulars. Those guys—and a few gals—who never got enough time on the mainframe.

Jason sat at the desk, overseeing the students working at their stations, occasionally helping them with a problem, but mostly reading. That was the *study* part of work-study that most departments got wrong. They worked their students ragged, leaving little time to read or do homework. In Physics, the job was monotonous, but also secondary. The exact opposite of the athletic department.

More than once, Jason thanked the stars he never took *that* bait in middle school. The coaches saw his size and athletic ability, first courting, and then haranguing him to join their programs. Too many of his friends in school fell victim to the pitch, and he rarely saw them after the beast swallowed them up. Most were now working in menial jobs, without a decent education, ground up by the football machinery of the state. A few got athletic scholarships to small universities. There they would again be sacrificed to the football gods for four or five years and *still* not have a marketable education to show for their troubles.

Jason closed his book in disgust after reading the same passage for the third time. It was Hugh Everett's *The Theory of the Universal Wavefunction*, and needed all his attention to understand it. Everett was an early pioneer in cosmology, though he left the field soon after publishing the thesis in Jason's hands. He tossed the book to the desk, and reached for another, more recent book from the stack. This one, Roger Penrose's *Shadows of the Mind*, was one he read in high school. It was only in the last year he had gained enough grounding in quantum theory to understand everything in it.

He was on the right track, he thought, *but Everett's right... I think the wave function* doesn't *collapse to a single state.*

Jason agreed with Penrose on one topic, though—artificial intelligence was a dead end. Most of his friends in computer science thought otherwise, and would debate him on this until late in the night. *Dan thinks we will all one day bow to our robot overlords*, Jason thought with a smile. *Of course, Dan also thinks Hogwarts is a real place.*

He checked the clock on the wall. "'Bout time to call it a night, guys. Start saving your work and shutting things down." There were a few groans from the far end of the room where a group gathered around a single monitor, but most packed their books and papers. He tossed the second book on the desk near the first and stood to stretch his legs.

As he stepped away from the desk, he glanced to where the two books lay and stopped. He reached down and turned them, lining them up side by side and shifting his gaze from one to the other. Back and forth, over and over, while his mind raced.

"Ha!" he almost yelled. "That's it!"

The students looked up to see what the commotion was about, but Jason was already sitting again and grabbing for a pencil and paper. After almost an entire semester of hand-wringing, he now had the subject for his senior honors thesis. Jason had almost given up hope he would find a suitable subject, several of his lesser ideas already rejected by his adviser.

Everyone smiled at him, shook their heads, and walked quietly out of the room. This wasn't the first time they witnessed such a reaction from an upper-level undergrad, and Jason knew each one prayed it wouldn't take *them* this long to figure it out.

***

"I'm telling you, Dan... this is it!" Back in his dorm room, surrounded by piles of notes and books, Jason sat on the edge of his chair. Dan had just walked into the room from a night of playing pool when Jason forced him to sit and listen.

"Can it at least wait until I'm sober?" Dan whined, sitting on the edge of his bed and struggling to pull off his shoes and socks. After a few tugs the second shoe came off, nearly hitting him in the head, and he dropped everything to the floor. They joined the growing mound of discarded clothes in the to-be-washed pile. He stared at the collection like he expected them to dance.

"Nah. You're in the *exact* state of mind to hear this," Jason said, grinning. "It's pretty out there."

"Dude... it's almost one, and I've got an early class tomorrow."

"Then you shouldn't have stayed out late and gotten liquored up."

Dan eyed Jason for a long time, eyelids straining under some unseen weight, and then scrubbed his face with both hands. "Okay, roomie," he said, waving his hand in a *gimme* gesture, "shoot."

"It has to do with why there will probably never be true self-aware artificial intelligence," he began.

"Ah hell, Jay, are we gonna have that argument again? 'Cuz let me tell ya, I think I'd rather sleep."

"Notice I said *probably* this time. I'll lay out the conditions for it in a bit, but first..." he picked up the two books he had been reading in the lab and held them out to Dan. After a few seconds Dan snorted and snatched them from Jason's hand. "Penrose says there can't be true artificial intelligence because what's happening in the human brain is quantum-related and can't be replicated in silicon."

"I've heard this shit before, buddy. What else ya got?"

"It also means even a quantum computer couldn't pull it off because we are still dealing with algorithms that *mimic* intelligence, and since real consciousness is rising from a purely non-algorithmic collapse to a single state, it won't work."

"And I still say Penrose is full o' shit."

Jason held his hands in front, waving them like a carnival barker as he spoke. "Here's the cool part," he pointed at the second book. "Everett there says the quantum wavefunction *never* collapses to a single state."

"Yeah, I know," Dan said, sobering. "That's the multiple worlds interpretation guy, right?" He sneered and shook his head. "What's one thing got to do with the other?"

"What if they're *both* right?"

Dan tilted his head and raised an eyebrow, almost falling over in the process. "I'm not sure I follow. How can two mutually exclusive ideas be both right?"

"Here's where my genius shines! Because the wavefunction only collapses *locally*." Jason stood, his body quaking with a barely restrained energy. Dan looked up at him, his eyes unfocused and uncomprehending. Jason paced as he spoke. "It's like this... all the quantum realities exist like branches on a tree, each decision marking a new path. The decision that marks the branch is the outward expression of a wavefunction collapsing to a single state, but the branching itself represents the universal wavefunction which *never* collapses!"

"So...?"

"What else looks like branches on a tree?"

"Um..."

"Jesus, Dan. You, of all people should—"

"A network!"

"Got it in one," Jason said, grinning. "Or infinity. Depends on your point of view, I guess," he said, rubbing the two-day stubble on his chin. "Penrose believes there's a quantum effect in the rise of intelligence and consciousness, and he's correct, but wrong in the process. I think maybe it's all about the network. From the day you are born—earlier, really—you make choices, branching off new universes with a version of yourself in each one. A you for every possible decision you could have made. But the branches constitute a network in a massively parallel quantum computer that is the source of sentience." He took a deep breath, "That's where the *you* comes from. Our consciousness arises naturally from the growth of the network."

"Are you sure?"

Jason laughed and sat on his chair again. "Oh, *hell* no. I'm pulling most of this straight out of my ass." He swiveled in the chair to pull some papers off the desk behind him. "Some of these concepts have already been explored in other papers I've found." He held up a sheaf, waving it behind him a Dan, "Albert and Loewer", then another, "H. Dieter Zeh. All pointing to what they call the many minds interpretation." He bent to the desk and snagged a pencil. "I'll have to change my whole schedule for next year, *and* take a couple of extra classes this summer. The math alone..."

Soon he was muttering to himself as he worked out an outline for his approach, Dan snoring like a chainsaw behind him.

***

"What did you mean last night about the conditions for AI?" Dan was pulling clothes from the "clean" pile beside his bed, taking a sniff, then laying them out for inspection. Occasionally he rejected one after the initial sniff and tossed it to the "to be washed" pile on the other side. Not a single piece had ever seen the inside of the dresser, as far as Jason knew, and the system—while odd and disorganized—worked for Dan.

"So you weren't completely out of it," Jason said with a grin. He had showered and dressed before Dan woke, and was already working on his outline again. The fact he hadn't slept never crossed his mind.

"Not *completely*, no," he said, rubbing his head. For Dan, this was known as "combing his hair." Little more than stubble most of the time, the jet black matte refused to do much more than just lay there. Dan scrounged in the nightstand next to his bed, pulled out a bottle of ibuprofen, and popped two in his mouth. "I clearly remember," he said around the pills, "you saying something about certain conditions allowing for an AI to be conscious."

Jason set the pencil down on the stack of papers and swiveled his chair to face his friend. "If that AI, even algorithm-based, is running in a quantum computer and allowed to make its own decisions, then it's a *possibility*." He tapped Penrose's book beside him for emphasis. "There are physical structures—microtubules—in the human brain that, in *theory*, operate on a quantum level. It's my hypothesis they could be responsible for the network connections throughout the multiverse that give rise to consciousness. If those structures can be mimicked in hardware..." he raised his hands and shrugged his shoulders.

"*Can* they be mimicked?"

"Haven't a clue. It's out of my field."

"Probably out of mine, too," Dan said, shaking his head. "I'm just a computer science geek, and I have a feeling this is gonna be way more complicated than your typical IT troubleshooting."

Jason chuckled. Dan was always selling himself short. *Like he actually believes the image he projects of himself.* "Not every computer science geek has read Penrose or Everett," Jason said.

"I blame you, roomie," Dan said with a short laugh, then grabbed a pillow and threw it like a frisbee at Jason's head. Instead it bounced off his chest and fell to the floor near the "to be washed" pile.

"You're gonna know even more before I'm through," he said with a wink. "I've gotta bounce my ideas off *someone*."

"What about Kat?"

"I try not to talk about this stuff around her. Puts her right to sleep."

"I don't know, Jay," Dan said, rubbing his head again, "Maybe a biology major would be of some use to you, donchathink?"

He hadn't considered that. Physics bored Kat to tears, and was a lousy topic of conversation on a date. After the first few times he tried to talk about his classes, watching her eyes glaze over, he avoided the topic like health-food. Now there was a possibility of overlap. He needed a lot of information in the field of biology—specifically the human brain—and that just happened to be Kat's focus. If nothing else, she could at least guide him to the right sources. Internet searches only went so far.

"I'll take the silence and the stupid look on your face as a yes," Dan said, watching him. "Personally, I think yer full 'o shit, but what do I know?" he said with a shrug. He dressed in slow motion, careful not to move around too much, then sat on the edge of the bed and bent to retrieve a shoe. "Ah, hell," he said, then ran out of the room and down the hall to the communal bathroom. The sounds of retching reached Jason's ears, but none of the odor made it through the door. After several minutes and two or three flushes, Dan staggered back inside. The color had leached from his face, but he stood a little straighter.

Jason gave him an evil grin. "Ready for breakfast?"

Dan's face twisted, turned a dull green, spun on his heels, and ran back the way he came.

"I would feel sorry for you," Jason yelled at his back, "but I seem to remember you serving me runny eggs the last time I was in your shoes."

The retching was louder this time.

***

Miles Henderson scraped the last of the eggs from the plastic plate and shoved the fork into his mouth. The other students at the table had just begun their meal, but Miles learned early in the Navy to shovel it in fast. He finished his one and only hitch three years ago, but those lessons suffered a slow death.

Something they have in common with my dad, he thought as he chewed. That was long behind him, and if the cops hadn't connected the dots by now, they never would. The fact he joined the Navy two weeks after his father disappeared hung a big red *arrest me* sign around his neck, but small-town Texas constabulary being what it was, they were still trying to figure out how to spell his name.

Keeping his temper in check during his time in the Navy was a simple task after living with his daddy. He mastered early the required attitude of obsequious deference to his so-called "superiors." Mastered it well enough to reach the rank of Petty Officer, 3rd Class—his CO even offering him 2nd Class just for re-upping—but the first four were more than enough for Miles. Enough to sock away as much cash as he could, and earn his GI Bill benefits.

Three years at Lamar University, in that dank armpit of a city known as Beaumont, he had enough left over from the GI Bill stipend and his savings to pay for a Masters. A year from now he would join the class of 2014 and graduate with a degree in Poly-Sci, then slide into a graduate program in Public Administration. For the first time in his life, things were looking up. Volunteering at his local congressman's campaign headquarters earned him the connections he desired most, and there was already a position waiting for him when he graduated.

"Hey Miles, what's got you smilin' today?" Bill Oaks poked at Miles at every opportunity, always on the lookout for the man's temper, and for some unfathomable reason disappointed every time the bait was ignored.

"Nothing you would understand, *Billy*." Miles' grin broadened as the other man stiffened. Bill Oaks hated being called Billy. "Just contemplating world domination."

The others laughed, some at Miles—but a couple at Bill—and Miles gathered his trash and stood. "Sorry boys, I've got a fact-finding tour today at the Exxon plant," he winked. "Can't keep the congressman waiting, you know."

"You still volunteering for that asshole?" another boy asked.

"Yep, and for as long as it takes," Miles said. He walked a couple of steps, then turned and said, "I've got your US

History paper ready for you, Billy, if you've got the cash." He smiled down at him, and the boy's face reddened. "Catch ya later."

He wouldn't. The fire at the refinery later that morning would see to that.

ERGO SUM

"**W**HY WON'T YOU EVEN DISCUSS IT?" JEAN STOOD NEAR Mikal's favorite chair, arms crossed over her chest and tapping her foot. Her eyes were moist and red.

"We *have* discussed it, Jean. More times than I can count." Forty-seven to be exact, but years of married life taught Mikal Weston that precision in the middle of an argument was unwise.

"I don't understand how you can be so cold. So unfeeling."

The tapping grew louder, matching the intensity of the pulse pounding in her neck. Mikal cataloged the symptoms of his wife's frustration without thinking. "I thought we settled this years ago," he said, measuring his words for just the right amount of calm. "Why must you keep bringing it up?"

"Why do I...?" she started. "Oh, you are such a... a... *robot*."

A robot, he thought. Others had called him such, but never his wife. He believed she saw inside him better than anyone, but on this one subject empathy failed her; she was blinded by a desire he couldn't comprehend. In her fury she cut him far worse than anyone had.

He spun on his heels, and without another word stalked out of their modest home, bypassing the usual lunch bag she

179

had prepared for him. In a final petty act, he left the door open.

*****

"Good morning, Dr. Weston," the office AI said.

"Good morning Alex. What do you have for me today?"

"Scans detect twelve quantum signatures. Two are beyond range, and eight are degraded below twenty percent." This was what Mikal loved most about his work—there was no wasted motion or useless chit-chat from the AI, and the morning's unpleasantness evaporated like springtime fog. He snapped open his data scroll and flattened it on the smooth and uncluttered surface of his desk. With access to Alex, the scroll displayed a wealth of information.

"This signal you have designated beta is exceptionally strong."

"True, sir, and not likely to add much to your research, but I calculate a ninety percent probability alpha will remain nearby for the next four hours."

"Plenty of time to give beta the once-over." Mikal gathered his data scroll and strode toward the research station and the already glowing Tank, a clear polycarbonate cube enclosing a volume of thirty cubic meters in the center of the room. Against the back panel of the Tank was a small bench, over which were three small hooks, each holding a disposable jumpsuit. A column of water a meter in diameter and two meters tall stood suspended in a containment field above a metal floor grate.

"Field emitters are charged, and all power leads are stable."

"All right, Alex," Mikal said with more calm than he felt. "Let's take a look."

"Very well."

Mikal chewed his bottom lip. Whether success or failure, he was committed. He heard a muffled pop as sub-atomic particles in the mass of water instantly re-aligned themselves, relinquishing their will to the trapped quantum signature, imposing new structure on old matter. A microsecond after the field performed its magic, the suspension field snapped off, and the remaining water cascaded through the grate to the holding tank, leaving a large naked man shivering on the floor.

The man coughed and sputtered, then looked down at his naked body and stood. "What the hell just happened?"

"There are three jumpsuits on hooks behind you," Mikal said. "Choose the one that fits best."

The man stared at Mikal for several seconds, then explored his surroundings. "What the hell happened?" he repeated.

"What is the last thing you remember?"

"I remember riding in my car and getting hit by a truck." As he spoke, he moved toward the door and placed his hands on the clear surface, peering intently beyond to the equipment in the outer room. As his hands explored, his face fell. "Why is there no handle on my side?" His eyes bored into Mikal, who adjusted his collar and stepped back.

"Do you know what year this is?" The man ignored him. Mikal stood at the control station drumming his fingers on the top. "Alex, do you have facial recognition on him?"

"Yes, sir. There is a ninety-nine percent probability he is James Clarke, born in Texas in 1992. Records indicate the accident to which he refers occurred in 2049."

Damn, Mikal thought. *Too recent, and not a large enough time frame.* The good news was there was still the alpha signal to test, and time enough to reset the Tank.

"Alex, please prepare for field shutdown."

"I'm dead, aren't I?" the man said, once again standing at the door.

Mikal narrowed his eyes, brow furrowing. This was the first time in eight years of research a subject realized his situation so early in the procedure. "Hold please, Alex." The test subject stood like a statue, arms limply at his sides, with his head tilted slightly. "Mr., uh... Clarke. I'm sure you have a great many questions, but—"

"You're going to shut me down. Or turn me off, or whatever you do to end me." He leaned forward, his eyes searching Mikal's face for answers. Mikal reeled, stepping back. This is far too early in the process for such a leap of logic.

"How long?"

"Mr. Clarke—"

"How long have I been dead?"

Mikal sighed and steeled himself for what he needed to do. Something about his face must have indicated an answer, however, as the other man's eyes grew wide, and he slumped to the floor.

"I was hoping..." His voice broke as his eyes filled with tears, quiet sobs escaping his throat.

Mikal watched Clarke's sudden collapse, incapable of comprehending the display of raw emotion. He knew of nothing that could so easily bring such a man to tears. Mikal could end both Clarke's pain and his own discomfort by dampening the field, returning the matter in that mass of flesh, blood, and bone to its original state. Instead, he was mesmerized by this outpouring. For an eternity of seconds, he observed the subject sitting on the floor, wondering what could have triggered such a swell of emotion.

Chest heaving, the man who was once James Clarke tried to speak. "I was just a... little late. Late... to the... ballpark." Gradually, the outburst quelled, and James sat on the floor of the Tank, sniffing and rubbing his eyes. "I promised my boy I would be there." He looked up at Mikal with heavy lids and reddened orbs floating on a shallow sea that threatened to spill over in a renewed wave. "I never even saw the truck until I was halfway through the intersection. That shit isn't supposed to happen anymore, anyway." He drew a sleeve across his face, and groused, "Self-driving cars my ass."

Mikal placed the data scroll on the surface of the control station and stepped toward the Tank, hands clasped behind his back. "To answer your first question—yes, you died in that accident." He stopped short of the Tank and his shoulders slumped. "To answer the second, the records indicate it occurred nearly fifty years ago. And that is a problem for me."

"Fifty years?"

"Nearly that. As I was saying, that is a problem for my research."

"Research? Is it cloning?" James lifted himself from the floor, looking down at Mikal.

"History, actually." Mikal straightened his back and lifted his chin. "I'm a historian."

James tilted his head and raised an eyebrow. "Historian. But..."

"Some time ago researchers discovered that which you might call a soul was both real and measurable. Everything we are—including memories—persists after death in the form of a single quantum state. These quantum signatures are all around us, but never interact with the physical world. They are nothing more than clumps of information. Construction plans, if you will."

"So, someone learned how to use these... plans?"

Mikal nodded. "Under the right conditions we impose a quantum signature onto a quantity of matter, recreating the subject as they existed just prior to death."

James rolled his shoulders, flexed his fingers, and said, "So how come I'm not all smashed up? I should be in pain from the accident, right?"

"That's something we still don't understand. The people we bring back in this way seem to be an idealized version of their previous state—perfect in every way, though still at the same age and general appearance they were when they died."

James looked down at his left leg. "Wow." He looked down at his legs, turning one this way and that. "I used to have a really nasty scar on my calf here from a motorcycle accident." He grinned. "Sucker's gone now. Better than plastic surgery."

"You'll also notice that your memory is eidetic—at least for a time—and every event in your life, everything you've ever seen, done, or heard is available for my research."

James looked into Mikal's eyes, a glimmer of hope emerging. More than that, there was something else—a strength and determination that Mikal remembered seeing in his father, though never in his own mirror.

"Unfortunately, Mikal said, "I can't use you."

And just like that, hope died. Murdered by mere words.

"Can't use me? Why not?"

Mikal sighed. "Please, Mr. Clarke, take a jumpsuit from the hook and I'll explain." James pursed his lips, then selected the largest of the three.

"Can I get a towel to dry off first?"

"Unnecessary. The jumpsuit will take care of that."

As James placed his legs into the jumpsuit and worked his upper body into the opening, water poured off the outside of the material in sheets. By the time he finished dressing, both his body, and the jumpsuit were completely dry. The opening in front closed seamlessly.

James sat and passed his hand over the cloth. "Well, I guess that's pretty cool," he muttered.

"As I was explaining, I've been collecting information from people such as you for the last eight years in an attempt to gather more accurate historical data of known events."

"That makes sense. Get the story straight from the people who were there. So, what's your time frame?"

"My main interest is the Cold War era. There are many things about that time that are still unknown, and most of the records have been lost or destroyed."

James seemed to consider this for a few seconds. "So you're saying that since I don't have direct memories of that time then I can't help you."

"Exactly."

"But what about indirect information? Stories I read or were passed down to me. That's gotta be—"

Mikal waved him to silence, as if dispersing a cloud of smoke. "They are neither reliable, nor useful. There are mountains of documents and research using indirect evidence, but little from the primary actors involved. While I have resurrected over twelve thousand people, I have only interviewed six direct participants in the governmental decision-making process. I have no control over who drifts into this chamber." He held his hands out and shrugged his shoulders. "It's completely random."

"So, when you turn off the field..."

"Your quantum signature will drift away. Most likely for good."

James lowered his head, examining his hands. "What if I don't want to go? Would you just kill me anyway?"

"Irrelevant," Mikal said, waving his hand dismissively. "You are already dead. In the eyes of the law, I'm talking to a recording right now."

The man in the cage looked up, eyes aflame, though his voice remained under quiet control. "I need to speak to my son."

"Mr. Clarke, you aren't in any position—"

"Alex, is it?" The question boomed from his chest as he lunged to the edge of the Tank, and it rang like a bell from the impact.

"Sir?" Alex replied.

Mikal rocked back and looked quizzically around the room as the AI responded directly to the subject. Another first.

"Is my son still alive?"

"The records indicate he is."

Again, the man looked at Mikal, the yearning in his eyes clear even to him. He made an obvious attempt to calm himself and said, "Please. I need to speak to my son. That boy was everything to me, and I left him without ever saying goodbye."

"Mr. Clarke, I'm sure he could handle the pain of losing a father at his age. You were fifty-seven when you died. He must have been at least—"

"Eight years old."

"But..."

A wan smile crept across James' lips. "Let's just say I was late to the game."

"Late to the...?"

James relaxed his shoulders, his hands fell to his sides, and he sighed. "I was forty-nine when my son was born. I started my family later than most, and for the life of me I can't imagine why I waited."

Mikal leaned his back against the control station and sighed. *This is maddening. I simply don't have time for such maudlin diversions.* And yet, in all the years and with all the subjects, James was the first to spark an interest outside of research. The man was so much like his own father, all emotion and action, yet so alien.

"You know why you waited. Your memory is perfect."

James chuckled softly. He sat on the bench and shrugged at Mikal. "Sure, I had all the regular excuses. Freedom, money, time. I convinced myself that my wife and I were happier that way. Then she left me, and I found someone much younger—as men at my age do from time to time." Another smile. "And after we married, Kathy told me she wanted kids right away—because of my age, and all. She said she wanted the children to grow up with a father. Maybe see a couple of grandkids before I die. So, I agreed. You know... just to keep her happy." He wrung his hands absently as he spoke, grinding them mercilessly against one another, but his eyes were so clear they shined. "And that made all the difference in the world. The day that boy was born I fell in love with him and fatherhood and never looked back." He wrapped his arms around his chest, hugging himself tightly, his eyes brimmed with fresh tears. "I can feel it even now," he breathed.

Mikal just stood and stared, finally remembering to breathe, watching this man quietly weeping—sometimes laughing—and rocking on the bench before him as recollections both joyous and aching flashed across his face in sweeping waves. Every question, every comment, died on

Mikal's lips before the asking. But he couldn't stand there all morning watching this man relive his memories.

In the end, Alex broke the spell.

"Dr. Weston?"

"Not now, Alex." *Why did I say that?*

"The alpha signal is drifting, and will soon be outside the capture zone."

Damn. "How long?"

"Approximately thirty minutes, sir."

James stared up at him. There was a fierce determination in his eyes, and the man's frustration was palpable.

Mikal took in a long slow breath and sighed heavily. "I'm afraid we're out of time Mr. Clarke." For the first time in his career, he looked a man squarely in the face and informed him of his fate. "I must move on before the signal drifts out of range." Under the other's steady gaze, eyes boring deep into Mikal's heart, he withered and deflated, the constant pressure a growing weight on his chest. "I'm sorry," Mikal whispered. "Truly, I am."

"But I'm not ready." Not a complaint or a cry, but a simple statement of fact.

"Alex, if you would..."

As he waited for the inevitable change from man to cascade of water, he offered him the courtesy of not turning away. It was a small thing, but too often Mikal dismissed his subjects out of hand without a thought, checking the next item off his list. It was demeaning, and until this moment, it had never bothered him.

"Isn't there a way to keep me here while you bring in the next subject?"

"It doesn't work that way. The Tank is designed to work with a single subject at a time. I'm not even sure how to modify the design to work as you suggest."

"Well, I don't want to go." Flatly. Again.

Mikal stepped back to the control station, running one hand through his hair while pinching the bridge of his nose with the other. There was no more time to waste, and no more patience with which to do it. "Alex, I asked you to turn off the field generator. Please do so now."

"Sir, I powered down the generator twenty-four minutes ago, when you first indicated Mr. Clarke was not a suitable subject."

With a start, he realized the low-level background hum that filled his ears for the past eight years was absent, the sheer volume of that silence a hole in the sound-scape. And yet, there stood James Clarke, impossibly grinning at him, with as feral a look as Mikal ever saw in another human.

James crossed his arms. "I told you, I'm not ready to go."

"Alex, is there a malfunction?" Mikal grasped at straws, and he knew it.

"No sir. The field is off. I believe there is precedent for this."

Of course there was. This was a known effect, but it rarely lasted for more than a second or two. James Clarke was holding himself together through sheer force of will, and the fact he held on this long was a marvel of determination. He couldn't keep it up, but the clock was ticking on the alpha signal.

Mikal's face puckered. "You won't be able to maintain this for long, you know. Even if you remain stable for days, you will eventually need sleep. Once you lose consciousness and its grip on the matter that makes up your body, the matter will revert to its former state. I could anesthetize you and end it now, but I'm curious how long you can maintain this." Mikal straightened a bit, looking not unlike a proud father. "So far, you have the record."

"Cool. I'm number one." James' eyes narrowed. "Now open the fucking door."

"What would be the point of—"

"Look, if you let me out you can reset this machine and work on your next subject while I sit here and wait to die." James' face softened a bit, and he shrugged his shoulders. "Besides, I'm hungry."

"Feeding him is contra-indicated, sir."

"Why is that, Alex?"

"Yeah. Why is that?" James was grinning again, but this time the mirth was real. He apparently realized something that Mikal did not, and that galled him.

"Feeding you requires opening the Tank." For the second time today, Alex was speaking directly to the test subject. *I should have a technician check the AI's programming,* Mikal thought. "The less obvious reason," Alex continued, "is that while the matter that constitutes your body is under the control of your will, any food you consume is not. Your body will process the food normally until your signature loses control, and the matter reverts to water. The food, however, will fall to the floor in whatever stage of processing is taking place at the time."

"Yuck," James said, wrinkling his nose.

"Indeed."

This is just intolerable, Mikal thought.

"And Dr. Weston?"

"Yes, Alex," Mikal sighed.

"You may have to rethink your idea of anesthetizing Mr. Clarke."

Mikal's squeezed his eyes shut and pinched the bridge of his nose again. "I'm afraid to ask, but why?"

There was a slight hesitation before Alex answered. Not much, but enough that it was clear Alex was accessing a huge amount of data, most likely from the law databases on the government servers, and they were notoriously slow.

"I believe this is, legally, a bit of gray area, sir. Since Mr. Clarke's existence is no longer dictated by the field, his status has changed regarding his human rights. While he is not a citizen, he is now an autonomous human being with all the concomitant rights."

"Oh, balls!" Mikal's jaw clenched, and he threw his hands in the air. "So now we just sit here and wait for him to destabilize? I have a schedule to keep!"

"Or you can let me out," Clarke said calmly as his eyes twinkled at the frustrated little historian.

"Or I can let you out," Mikal agreed as he rolled his eyes skyward and shook his head. He knew he could wait the man out. In the long run, the laws of quantum mechanics were on Mikal's side. In the near-term, however, there was still the alpha signal. If he wanted to get any real work done today, he must clear the Tank and reset for the capture of that signal. Clarke could hold on for a few seconds, or minutes—even hours—and there was nothing to do but wait. It was a gamble with purely random variables.

Mikal hated gambling.

His shoulders slumped, arms hanging limply at his sides, resigned to the choice he made. "Alex," he said wearily, "would you..."

Mikal's ears popped lightly as the seal on the door to the Tank broke, equalizing the pressure between the room and the Tank. He looked up at James Clarke standing sheepishly half in and half out, his right hand pressing lightly against the inner surface of the door. He took a slow breath, shook off his hesitation, and stepped confidently through. It was an unprecedented event; a subject had never left a Tank in all the history of the device.

He took several steps, stopped and looked around the room as if for the first time, then turned to Mikal, placing his hands on his hips. "Now what?"

Mikal snorted and pointed with little enthusiasm to a chair against the far wall. "Now you sit over there and keep out of my way while I do my job."

James walked toward the chair, but instead of sitting, he leaned his back against the wall and crossed his arms. Mikal's eyes followed him, and when he was satisfied James was no longer an immediate concern, he nodded once and turned back to the control panel.

"Reset the Tank, Alex."

"Yes, sir." As soon as the door closed, the lock activated and a fine mist emerged from both the floor and the ceiling, shrouding the interior with an impenetrable fog. Within seconds, powerful fans whisked all traces of the fog from the Tank. Water poured from the ceiling and coalesced into a thick column. The field generator spun up, its low hum filling the room.

"Sir, the field is at full strength."

"Initiate capture."

Mikal eyed James as he leaned away from the wall, the man's entire body a coiled spring of potential energy focused on the Tank. Mikal turned his attention back to the water. There. Right in the center of the water column, a flash of pink skin. A light popping noise, a brief burst of light, a body lying naked on the floor, and then... nothing. The column of water fell through the grate, leaving nothing but a memory of what had once been.

"Damn!" Mikal slammed his fist on the top of the console. "An entire day... wasted."

"What did you do?" James cried out.

"Nothing, Mr. Clarke. Not a damn thing. The signal wasn't useful, so we let it go."

Something in his eyes forced James to draw back from him. There was hardness, but it wasn't real. "What do you mean? I saw him! There was a child right there on the floor!"

"Correct, sir," Alex answered before Mikal opened his mouth. "Protocol dictates a child under the age of twelve is not to be reconstituted, and I calculated this child's age at approximately six years old."

"But he was alive."

"Three thousand, forty-two." Mikal muttered beneath a long sigh.

"What?"

"Three thousand, forty-two." He raised his head to peer into James' eyes, "That's how many times I've..." He lowered his chin. "It doesn't get easier with practice." His chest was a hollow void filling with pain and anger. "And once I overrode the protocols." He looked away, shame and anger heating his cheeks. "I won't do that again. Ever."

James looked at Mikal with something approaching pity, then his faced hardened to granite. "It's wrong to just give and take life without at least giving them a chance," he growled.

Mikal gently placed a hand on James' shoulder. "It would have been cruel." He looked up into the man's eyes, holding both himself and the other steady with his gaze. "That child's life in the Tank would have been short, lonely, and terrifying. Think about it, man." A look from James, and Mikal dropped his hand from the shoulder. "I can't do that again. I won't. It... it hurts." He never thought about it in those terms, really. Always before, the justification was the protocols, but even then he knew he was lying to himself.

James lowered his eyes. "But he could have been like me. He could have—"

"James," Mikal shook his head, "*no one* is like you."

The light patter of dripping water was the only sound in the room, but it didn't all come from the Tank. James sniffed twice, rubbed his eyes, and raised himself again to his full height.

"I need to see my son." Even as his voice broke and caught in his throat, there was a growing strength. "It's been too long."

Mikal stood there for long seconds, immobile, while a storm raged in his head. Years of arguments with torrents of tears played like a looped video within his mind, all of it preparing him for this moment, the whole of his life falling neatly into place. It was a revelation that hit him full in the gut. James opened his mouth, but Mikal stopped him. "I know."

"You know what?"

"It's time for you to go." The decision made, Mikal burned with a need to act. He retrieved his data scroll from the console. "You'll need this." He placed it in James' hands. "Most people have ID chips implanted in their forearm for identification and monetary transactions, but some old-timers still use their personal data scroll."

"I don't understand."

Mikal grinned. "I'm setting you free. Kicking you out of the nest. Tossing you out into the cruel world, as it were."

"But—"

"Nope. I've made up my mind." Giddy and manic, Mikal walked toward the door. "Alex, transfer ownership of my data scroll to Mr. Clarke, but keep the financial and identification information intact and available"

"Of course, sir. Transfer complete."

"There you go," he said as he turned back to James. "You'll have full use of this scroll, including access to my finances while you search for your son. Don't go crazy, though." He shook a finger in James' face. "I am not a wealthy man. I believe you can get anywhere in the world in two days, so Alex will deactivate the device then. Fair enough?"

As Mikal lowered into his desk chair, James waved the data scroll in his direction. "I don't know how to use this thing."

"No worries. Touch both corners of the exposed end." He watched James' eyes light up as he demonstrated, and the scroll snapped open and flat. He smiled again and his heart raced. "Ask it for help on whatever topic or function you need."

James looked at Mikal, grinning fiercely, and, speaking to the scroll, said, "Can you locate James Emerson Clarke the third, born June twenty-first, twenty forty-one, in Harris County, Texas."

"The third?" Mikal grinned.

James returned the look, but a bit sheepishly. "The wife's idea, okay?"

The data scroll spoke in a voice not unlike Alex. "Subject currently residing in Dallas, Texas. Location and mapped directions are displayed. Would you like to see an image?"

"Yes!"

Beneath the map appeared an ever-changing collage of pictures taken over the years—many from childhood, with both father and son—and James could no longer restrain the hope and longing as he wept openly. Mikal, finding his eyes wet as well, smiled up him.

***

Alex offered to track James' progress, but Mikal refused. As long as he didn't know, all possibilities were still available, and in at least one of those possible futures James would. Mikal could live his whole life without the certainty of a real outcome, and in ignorance there was hope. There was a brief instant of despair when he exited the building and noticed a large wet spot on the sidewalk just outside the door, but Alex assured him through the new data scroll that it was from the nearby garden sprinklers.

The bus slid to a glassy-smooth stop, and as soon as the doors parted, he stood and exited the cabin. He fumbled for a second as he tried to jam his hands in his coat pockets, then smiled as he remembered he'd given it to James. Still smiling when he walked in the door of his modest home, he found Jean sitting primly in his favorite wingback chair, her face in her hands, quietly crying.

Frozen in the doorway, the smile melted from his face, and the door closed silently behind him.

"Jean?"

The woman who loved him—had bothered to marry him—raised her face toward him, a host of questions behind her reddened eyes. Only one made it to her lips.

"Are you leaving me?"

Mikal straightened and staggered back as if struck. "What? I... No! Where did you get that idea?"

Jean took a ragged breath and held out her data scroll. "You were so angry this morning when you left, and then I saw you purchased a single transit pass to Dallas."

Mikal forgot himself and instantly knelt before her, reaching for the data scroll. The charge showed up less than an hour after James left. *He got that far, at least!* Without warning, Mikal jumped to his feet, carrying Jean with him in a hard embrace, letting out a cry of joy as she squealed in surprise.

When he finally set her down, the grin on his face, and the tears in his eyes promised a story he knew she had waited years to hear.

"Jean, there is so much to tell you about today!" Though the grin remained, his eyes softened. "But before that, I think we should talk about this morning."

"Mikal, stop right there," she said, pulling away. "I already know how you feel. You've made yourself perfectly clear."

"Look, I just want to ask you one question."

Jean crossed her arms, her eyes narrowing in growing suspicion. "And that would be?"

"If it's a boy," he smiled down at her, "can we name him James?"

Before he could prepare himself, she jumped in his arms, hugging him tightly around his neck. "But you always said—"

"I know," he said through his laughter.

Stepping back, she eyed him cautiously. "What happened to you today?"

"It's a long story, Jean, but I've come to some realizations about my life."

"But..." She looked up at him again, an alloy of hope and suspicion in her eyes.

Mikal breathed deeply and let out a long great sigh of contentment. "Let's just say I don't want to be late to the game."

I hesitated including this piece in this anthology. It is a depressing story of life in what should be a Utopia (think Universe 25), and is another bit of backstory for an unfinished novel. That book I began over ten years ago as a discussion of where we are as a society and where we are headed.

The novel has become distressingly prescient...

SUCH INDEED IS HOW THE STEADFAST ACT

JOE ANDERS WALKED OVER TO THE OLD 3D PRINTER AS IT rattled and buzzed, furiously making a new pair of sneakers. He bent to look at the display. *Damn*, he thought, *eight hours and still only sixty percent complete.* Checking the feed hoppers, he noticed there weren't enough raw materials left to finish the job. Joe sighed and stabbed at the pause button , praying to whatever deity was in vogue this week it restarted properly after refilling.

Outside his window, the rising noise from the street below leaked into his tiny apartment. The morning sun was just peeking between the buildings, but the city was awake and busy. *The protesting will begin soon*, he thought. It was as good as a a job for many, now. Protest from sunup to noon, break for lunch—provided by street vendors who ran food trucks owned by the mega-corps—and then march and protest more until sundown.

Lather, rinse, repeat.

With unemployment over fifty percent and rising, some people lived their entire lives without ever knowing a paying job. It was just background noise now. Few paid attention, and fewer still tried to do anything about it. The cops in riot gear watched from the sidewalks, each likely praying the protests didn't become violent.

Joe cocked his head as the sounds of the street changed. Louder than usual, it sounded like cheering—but there was another, angrier layer underneath. "Just keep the delays to a minimum, people," he said as he peered through the tattered curtain. "That's all I ask."

***

Joe stood on the curb beside a cop outside his building waiting for an opening in the crowd. This time of the morning, the wave was moving in the general direction of his job, so the important thing was to stay upright. Falling would make this a very bad day indeed. He smiled up at the big cop, who nodded once at him. The protective mask obscured the man's face, but Joe was certain it held no more emotion than the polycarbonate shield covering it.

"At least you guys will always have a job," Joe said.

The cop's shoulders slumped, and he pointed over the street. Joe turned his head and saw the armed drones hovering over the crowd.

"The newest units are autonomous." The cop leaned close and whispered, "Union rep's telling us that replacement through attrition has already started. Forced retirements are coming 'round the bend. After that..." He shrugged and stood back at attention.

Layoffs. Joe felt the word crawl up his spine. There were no temporary layoffs anymore.

"If you're headed to work, sir, I suggest you get there on time."

"Yeah," Joe agreed as he watched the protest. "I probably should, at that." He nodded at the cop and stepped off the curb.

At the next intersection he saw a figure working back the opposite direction. While the sea of flesh didn't exactly part, the person had little trouble navigating against the current. The cheering that Joe heard earlier followed the figure, along with a smattering of growls of anger.

As Joe drew near, he saw the person headed his way was a woman. Tall and slim, an almost boyish figure, with red hair and a white dress she was a tapered candle passing with regal austerity through the crowd. Her face, hair, and clothes were too perfect by half. Everything about her spoke of affluence even if her presence in the street did not.

As she approached Joe, he noticed the sheaf of papers she carried, passing them to people on the street. She reached out and placed one into his hands as she drifted by, smiling thinly at him. Joe turned to follow that vision, but the people closed ranks in her wake, and the crowd drove him ever forward. He heard another cry of joy and anger behind, and as he turned his head to catch a last glimpse of her, he stuffed the paper into his pocket.

Joe turned onto Billings, and the crowd thinned. Now able to walk at his own pace, he slowed as thoughts of her filled his head. *Got to be the most beautiful woman I've ever seen up close*, he thought. He noticed for the first time he was smiling. If only he knew her name! With that information he could...

Nothing. I could do... nothing.

Women like that didn't associate with men of his status. *Money follows money*, he thought. Shrugging his shoulders, he increased his speed. There was always a backlog waiting for him after a vacation.

***

When he arrived at the hospital, Carolyn, the day-shift receptionist, stood and looked up from her desk with a strange expression.

"I've only been gone two weeks. You can't have forgotten me already," Joe said with a smile as he passed by her station. She looked on the verge of saying something, then closed her mouth and sat again. Joe didn't have time for chit-chat, anyway. He still had to change into his scrubs and take inventory of the supplies for his shift, make sure every station was well-stocked, and see that the rest of the staffing was in place—all before the next wave of ambulances arrived. Most of the supplies comprised syringes filled with what the staff called Fix-It, but the containers of nano-bots from the world's only supplier were scarce in the city proper.

Joe accumulated a crushing debt becoming a doctor, and here he was ten years later little more than a technician. The only time he used his skills these days was when they ran out of Fix-It, or the problem was one of the few things it couldn't handle—what everyone in the emergency room called *meatball surgery.*

"Dr. Anders?" The voice behind him was as familiar as a headache.

"Bill," Joe said, and he swung to the grinning hospital administrator. Bill Graves rarely smiled, and when he did, it was almost exclusively while delivering bad news.

"I need you to come to my office," the little man said, hands clasped behind his back.

"I'm a little busy here, Bill. My shift's about to start." Joe turned toward the ER again, and walked away

202

from the unpleasant weasel, calling back over his shoulder, "Can we do this dance during my break?"

Graves followed, practically skipping. "Better yet, I think we can do it in the ER. It will save time."

"Fine, but just stay out of my way," Joe snapped. *Why do I let the little cypher get under my skin?*

Joe led the way to the locker room and changed into his scrubs while Graves waited with a thin smile stretched across his face. The man leaned against the wall by the door, arms crossed in a desperate attempt to look casual. Joe knew better. Graves was so tense Joe could have used him for an ironing board. Electric with pent-up energy, the stern set of his jaw told Joe he was in a hurry to get to the ER. Joe moved like he dressed for his own execution. He stuffed the last of his clothes into the locker and turned and walked out of the room without a word.

***

"What the hell?" Joe stared at the bare emergency room.

"I thought you'd like it." Bill Graves rarely smiled, but as Joe turned, the man was bouncing in delight, a ghoulish grin riding his face, and rubbing his hands like a housefly. "We had all this installed just last week."

Once there were a dozen beds and their accompanying medical carts at a dozen stations. In their place were what looked like large coffins without a cart or doctor or nurse in sight.

"Where are the beds? My damn staff?"

"No longer necessary." Graves waved his arm. "These are state-of-the-art Medi-Beds." Walking to the nearest, he pressed the single button on the surface. With a soft hiss, the coffin's top split and opened like a Venus Flytrap. "Everything is self-contained. Nano-bots for the most common issues, and robot surgeons for everything else." He turned and smiled again at Joe. "A single technician with minimal training can run this entire ER."

Joe's face was hot and he balled his hands into fists. "So now I'm officially downgraded to technician?"

"Oh no... you misunderstand," he said with all the charm of a snake, waving his hand dismissively. "I said minimally trained," he sniffed. "You, sadly, are over-qualified."

And then it hit him. Laid off.

Graves saw something on Joe's face, and he shrank back to place the coffin between himself and the doctor.

"N-now, Dr. Anders," he stammered as he held his hands up before him. "You must know there was nothing I could do."

"No, of course not." Joe was breathing heavily, on the verge of violence. *The little jerk is right*, he thought, forcing himself to calm. *This would have happened eventually. So what if the asshole is enjoying it?*

Joe sighed, and turned to leave, but couldn't resist a parting shot. "Don't be so smug," he said softly. "You're next." He watched the smile melt away from the weasel's face, but he felt no better.

***

"It's called an Enclave, Mr. Anders." The Unemployment Guidance Counselor sitting across from him was a prune-faced woman of indeterminate age. "It is currently a pilot project, but Congress just voted to create a full program." She peered at him over her reading glasses with practiced sincerity.

He studied the crumpled paper in his hands the woman in the street had given him. "What's the part about giving up my rights?"

204

"Well, you can't expect taxpayers to allow the... um... non-taxpaying members of society to have a say in how government spends its funds." Her eyes widened. "I mean, what's to keep them from taking over and voting themselves even more benefits. There are so many after all." She sniffed again as punctuation.

"Other than it's nearly impossible to vote as it is?" Joe said blandly.

"Be that as it may, you would give up only those things you rarely use anyway—the right to vote, assembly, and free speech." She waved her hand in the air as if dispersing a cloud of smoke.

"And in return, we get...?"

"Oh, wonderful things," she said, brightening. She ticked off each point on her fingers, "A new apartment sized to meet the needs of your family. Food, based on the same calculation. Free basic health care. Education for your children from the finest teaching software. Clothing... even furniture manufactured to order."

"But we can never leave?"

"Oh, no. Travel may be permitted between Enclaves— when and if they build others—but not to communities where taxpayers live." She looked over her glasses again, and said, "You understand, of course."

"Of course." *Out of sight, out of mind.* Joe stood, straightened his shirt, and held his hand out across the desk. "Thank you, ma'am, I think I've heard enough."

She looked at him over her glasses, and he let his hand drop to his side. Joe turned and left the tiny cubicle. On his way out, he passed dozens of these, each occupied by the unemployed or the soon-to-be unemployed. Hundreds of hopeful faces looked up at him as he walked, saw his expression, and dropped their gaze again to their hands in dismay.

***

"You should come with me. This'll be the protest of the year!" Gerald's voice carried across the small apartment from the computer to Joe's kitchen. His enthusiasm was ever-present, even in the face of his own layoff last year.

"I'm not much of a protest guy, Ger."

"Seriously, Joe, you should get out and shake off the misery for a while." Joe watched his friend lean forward into the camera. "I hear she's gonna be there."

"She, who?"

"Aw man, don't tell me you haven't seen Sati!" His eyes widened. "She's the only reason I go to these things. Some kind of rich debutante and totally committed to the cause." Gerald grinned and waggled his eyebrows. "A real looker, too. Makes me like redheads... and you know I'm a blondes-only guy."

***

The plaza in front of the courthouse was packed, but Joe didn't mind the pressing bodies around him. Barely able to hear Sati speaking from where he stood with Gerald, he wasn't paying attention to what she said, anyway. It was the way she moved when she spoke that interested him. Every motion was graceful, and... *planned*, somehow. She was a maestro conducting her orchestra.

"A buddy of mine invited us to the after-party," Gerald yelled in his ear over the cheers of the crowd. "You game?"

Joe turned an astonished face toward his rather slow-witted friend. "Are you kidding me? If she's there, I'm there."

Sati finished with raised arms, then lowered her head as the waves of cheers washed over her. Others on the makeshift stage rushed to hustle her off to parts unknown, but she stopped halfway down the steps and turned back to retrieve a stack of papers from the lectern. Her head dipped as she held the papers her chest, then scampered from the plaza.

"C'mon, Joe." Gerald pulled at Joe's shirt, dragging him through the crowd.

"Where are we going?"

Gerald pointed toward an old storefront, empty and shuttered, across the plaza. "There's a Vanara guarding the door, but I've got a note that should get us past."

"Should?"

Gerald smiled, and shrugged his shoulders. "Everything's a crapshoot, man."

"What happens if we come up snake-eyes?"

His friend snorted. "Then I guess we'll see what kind of skills you have when you don't have Fix-It backing you up."

Joe laughed nervously, but as they approached the Vanara, the laughter caught in his throat. He looked up at the hirsute creature and wondered why a sentry-bot hadn't replaced the modified human.

Gerald beamed and presented the note he held as if making an offering to the gods. "Mike invited us," he mumbled, shifting his weight from one foot to the other. Joe noticed the Vanara didn't move a muscle, his weight distributed over the balls of both feet.

The Vanara's eyes locked on Gerald, then shifted as he scanned the note with a prosthetic eye. Connected to the global network, that eye could identify any face, or analyze handwriting, fingerprints, and retina scans. It was a very expensive add-on.

Satisfied, he stepped aside. As Joe followed Gerald into the building, he heard the Vanara say, "Don't make me come in there to get you."

"Yes, sir," Joe squeaked.

Inside the building was quieter than the plaza, even with the furious discussion Joe heard from the back room.

"It's just unnecessary!" They entered the small, dimly lit room, and every pair of eyes turned toward them. Joe, however, saw only Sati; she sat on the tattered sofa and hugging her knees against her chest. The pure white dress she wore covered her from neck to ankles, but did nothing to hide her beauty. Her eyes were open, but she stared at the floor as if in a trance.

"Who the hell are you?" The man standing before Sati now directed his anger at the interlopers.

"You said..." Gerald began, his voice quivering, as another man jumped up to confront them.

"It's okay, Hank," Mike said. "They're with me." The man Joe assumed to be Hank stood to one side of the sofa, one hand resting on Sati's shoulder. The woman looked up at Joe, emerald eyes locking with his blue. She smiled weakly, and his face flushed and his heart raced.

"I've made up my mind," she said to Mike in a quiet and husky voice. "No one is talking me out of it, so please... just help with the planning."

Mike stood still as and ice sculpture for a few seconds, then the tension leaked out of him. His shoulders slumped, and he knelt before her. "Sati... please," he said softly.

"No, Mike. It's the only thing left," she said. Then softer, as Joe strained to hear, "And it's what I want."

Mike's chin fell to his chest, and he breathed heavily as the others held theirs. He looked up into her eyes, and when he spoke his voice cracked. "I will do as you ask." His gaze fell to the floor. "But I will not watch."

"I would never ask you to, brother." She patted his hand lightly, then her face brightened as she turned to Joe. "You are Joe Anders?"

She knows my name! Following quickly on the heels of that thought, another crept in. *Why does she know my name?* He turned to glare at Gerald, whose eyes were as wide as his own.

"Hey, Joe, I've got nothing to do with this," he said. "Mike told me there was going to be a party."

Joe realized he clenched his hands into fists and forced himself to relax. "Yes, I'm Joe Anders." He tilted his head and raised an eyebrow. "Is there a reason you brought me here?"

She smiled crookedly, a sad humor radiating from her face. "I'm afraid I need a doctor."

***

"Sure, I can modify the Fix-It with the right equipment, but I don't understand why."

Joe sat to the right of Sati, so close he could feel the warmth of her body. Her scent wafted his nostrils with every motion, disrupting rational thought. She reached up and brushed her flaming hair behind her ear, then laid her hand across his own.

"There is a large protest in two days, and I need the... um, endurance to see it through." Everyone around the table—other than Gerald—looked away or studied their drinks; Gerald tossed down drinks like they were his last.

Joe sneered at the idea. "What makes this one more important than the thousands of others?"

Sati drew her hand back to her lap. "The president will sign the relocation bill by the end of the month," she looked around the table, "and we mean to stop it."

Joe leaned back in his chair. "Isn't that supposed to be a good thing? People will no longer have to worry about jobs, or how they will live without one."

She smiled thinly at him. "The goals are laudable, but the method is contemptible. This is nothing more than an attempt to warehouse the poor and unemployed." Her voice rose in volume and tenor with every word. "That these people must give up their rights should be enough to tell you it's wrong."

"So how do you propose to fix it?" *Rich-girl guilt*, he thought.

Sati sighed, then slumped back in her chair. "What you may not know is that energy is now free and has been for years." Her eyes narrowed. "With that one advancement, the cost of all manufacturing comes down to the cost of labor and raw materials. With robots replacing humans for labor that means everything is effectively free." Everyone nodded their heads. "Don't you understand, Joe? This world should be a paradise!" She shook her head. "Instead, it's a nightmare." She placed her hand once again atop his. "We need to delay the president's signature long enough to change his mind."

Joe looked around the table and realized he was the only one here who could do what she wanted, but he didn't believe she couldn't find another. It was a simple thing she wanted after all. Fix-It was time-limited, repairing damage as directed and then flushed from the body. There was no technical reason why it couldn't keep working indefinitely since it drew power from the same processes driving cellular functions.

The reprogramming was easy for him, or anyone else with his years of experience with the beasties, and Joe was under no illusions he was the only doctor on her list—even if modifying Fix-it was wildly illegal. Sati told him all she wanted was for the Fix-It to keep her body operational while she performed a public filibuster.

Simple, really. *Too simple*, he thought. He was sure there was more to the story, but ultimately it didn't matter. *Let the rich sacrifice for a change.*

"Okay, I'll do it," Joe said with a shrug. Everyone else at the table released a long-held breath.

She leaned forward and brushed her full, red lips against his cheek. "Thank you," she whispered in his ear. When she pulled back, he saw tears in her eyes, but she was looking past him to her brother. Joe turned to see the man clenching his jaw beneath hot skin.

***

Joe looked at the four syringes on the table in front of him, each containing a single dose of Fix-It. The three glorious weeks spent with Sati while waiting for the group to buy the nanos was far too short. He'd been wrong about her—she really was committed to making the world a better place, but she was clearly both naïve and malleable; the group would never get a single dose, ending her plans before they began, but just as clearly he was wrong.

He stared at the glittering instruments. "Who gets the other three?"

Hank turned and nodded to Sati. "They're all for her." *There's that hand on her shoulder, again*, Joe thought.

"That's nuts, Hank," Joe said. "A single dose is enough."

Mike, on the verge of speaking, was interrupted by Sati's velvet voice. "I don't want to just stay upright, Joe. I need to be lucid for as long as possible." Mike sat, elbows on the table, and placed his head in his hands. She moved closer to Joe, touching him lightly on his shoulder. "I want two doses dedicated to brain function, and two for the rest of me. One of each held in reserve to take over after the first fails."

Joe straightened, "You're not making any sense." He sat, pulling her into the chair beside him. "I'm removing the time locks. There won't be any failure."

Mike pounded both his fists once on the table, stood and glared at Hank, then turned and stalked out of the room without a word. Sati's eyes glistened as she stared at her brother's back.

She sighed once, then turned again to Joe, smiling at him, full of warmth and—what looked to Joe's eyes— hope. "This will work, Joe. I know it." She wiped her eyes and smiled crookedly again. "Mike thinks it's a wasted effort. He may be right."

"I think he's right, too. Sati... no one has paid attention to these protests in years."

"They will to this one," Hank said with puffed–up pride. He saw the barely disguised contempt on Joe's face. "I have friends in the media. There will be cameras on Sati the whole time."

Sati looked at her hands. "I think I can hold their attention long enough for people to hear me."

They're using *her*, he thought. *Aren't we all?* "I guess I should get started." He looked at Hank. "Do you have the imprinting unit I requested?"

Hank nodded. "It's on the way." He looked at Sati, catching her eye for just a second, then said, "I'll go check on it."

Joe watched him leave the room, then turned back to Sati. "It shouldn't take me more than two hours to reprogram them once I have the right equipment."

She looked up at Joe, her eyes locking on his. Her face flushed. "If only..." she began, and then she was standing and hugging him with a fierce intensity. Her head tilted up as he looked into her eyes, and her lips found his. Her kiss was hungry, a lioness who had never known a meal, and Joe lost himself in her.

***

The sky was as blue and crystalline as Joe ever remembered, the air crisp and cool. *A perfect day*, Joe thought. The crowd swelled to gargantuan proportions, and the media were out in force—as were the cops and sentry-bots.

Sati stood at the edge of the stone steps in front of the courthouse, this time dressed in red, and on her it was nothing short of breathtaking. There was a solid semi-circle of people about ten meters in front of her, and from every direction no one was closer than that; even the Vanara stood watch stoically at that distance. Joe pressed through the crowd to get closer, and when he reached the edge, he felt a tingling on his skin. He tried to push beyond, but found he could go no farther than a few inches.

A personal barrier field? An invisible swarm of nano-bots surrounded the area around Sati. Moving faster than the eye could register, they interdicted any solid mass that tried to pass through.

Impressive. The barrier wasn't just expensive—it was impossible to get, reserved for military and government use. Or daughters of the ridiculously wealthy. In that bubble she might speak unmolested for an eternity. Hank had prepared for everything.

"To exist is not enough!" Amplified by the field protecting her, Sati's voice carried over the crowd, crashing through the thousands of murmuring souls and silencing them as it passed. "To consume, live, grow old, and die is not enough." She found Joe's eyes. "To love... is not enough."

She used me, he realized. *As surely as Hank is using her now.* Just as Joe planned to use her to help him find work—any work—after this day ended. He looked around the Plaza at the others of their group. Something's not right. Of all her entourage, only he and Gerald were facing her. Even the Vanara faced away. The Vanara. Joe noticed the man's face for the first time, and there was a look of... anguish. A resigned acceptance of pain.

"Long they have held you down, unable to enjoy the fruits of the garden this world has become." She held her arms wide, encompassing the mass of humanity in the plaza. "Now you must give up the last of your freedoms merely to exist."

Mike was nowhere among her small circle of friends, but Hank was at the top of the steps. Joe saw his face from where he was, and Hank was sobbing. He turned back to the Vanara and saw the tears streaming down the face of one of the most feared creatures in the city.

All at once, an unreasoning worry hit him, and Joe felt the urge to be near her. He pressed against the barrier, but it pressed back with equal force.

"Today I show you the truth. Better to die free than simply exist."

Joe looked up just as the hem of her dress burst into flame.

"No!" *Not like this. Not like this!* He ran to the Vanara and pounded on his chest. "What is she doing? Help her," he cried.

The flames licked at the folds, growing in strength as they crawled up the fabric. The closest ranks of the crowd stumbled back and cried out in alarm as earlier cheers of support transformed into growls of anger and confusion.

"We are all what we make of ourselves." The flames, having consumed the skirt, now feasted on her flesh. Her face registered the beginnings of the agony to come, but her voice never wavered. "Everyone has the right—the responsibility—to achieve all they can." Her hands clenched into fists, and she dropped them to her sides. "Don't allow yourselves to be herded like cattle to the slaughterhouse," she cried. Joe saw her legs blacken, but as she collapsed to her knees in pain, parts of the black flaked off to reveal pink new skin.

"Oh my God!" *Endurance.* He tried to run to her, but the Vanara grabbed his wrist in a massive hand, and nothing but a bullet to the man's brain would win Joe his freedom. "Someone, please... bring water," he yelled as loud as he could. "Anything!" The cops, once roused, moved to help, but were no more effective against the barrier than he. From overhead a stream of water blasted the barrier, but it evaporated on contact.

The flames grew higher, and Sati screamed.

And everyone on the plaza froze. Joe refused to give up, continuing the struggle against the Vanara's grip, but it was hopeless. At last he understood and stopped. The Vanara released him, then placed a heavy arm around Joe's shoulders.

Up on that top step, Sati burned. The nanos worked furiously to regenerate dying tissue while those in her brain kept her horribly lucid. It was a losing battle, and the air around her sparkled with dying nanos. Joe knew the average person would die in under four minutes so consumed, and the nerves registering pain would die long before that.

Sati was no average woman. She was pumped full of nano-bots dedicated to keeping her body alive and her brain functioning by any means necessary. Joe saw to that.

She screamed for twenty-seven long, sickening minutes.

***

"The president signed the bill an hour ago," Mike said. He stood behind Joe as he sat on the steps near the blackened concrete marking Sati's immolation. The plaza was uncharacteristically empty. "He saw her protest and wanted to make sure no one else did the same."

"So she died for nothing." Joe reached out to touch that stain—to stain himself. *If not for me...*

"Not nothing." Mike sighed and sat beside him. "She died thinking she made a difference. For some of us that's as good as it ever gets."

Joe turned to look into Mike's eyes, searching the man's face for the pain he felt. "Why did you let her do it?"

"Short answer?" He tilted his head, a wan smile on his lips. "Sati was a force of nature. You don't stand in front of a hurricane and expect to stop the thing."

A cleaner-bot trundled out of the courthouse, halted near the stain, and worked on removing it. Joe stood up and kicked it as hard as he could. The 'bot crashed to the bottom of the steps, righted itself, then wobbled to the back of the building.

"They'll just send another."

"I know. That's the eleventh one I've sent back."

Mike reached up, and Joe grasped his hand and pulled him to his feet. He turned and looked into Joe's eyes. "What will you do now?"

Joe looked away from the blackened stone and turned toward the building behind him. "I'll go see my Unemployment Guidance Counselor." He saw the quizzical look on the other man's face. "I'm taking the government up on its offer, Mike." He swept an arm around the plaza. "There's nothing for me here, now."

Mike's shoulders slumped. "Then Sati failed."

"No... there was never any chance of success. That's not the same thing." Joe shook his head, and the tears came for the second time that day. "Hank was a fool. He... *we* used her for a pointless display." Joe shoved his hands in his pockets as another cleaner-bot exited the building, "Like you said, Mike, some things can't be stopped." He turned and walked toward the courthouse, the bot passing him on its way to do its job.

This story is also loosely related to both the previous short story and the unfinished novel, and while also a bit of a downer, I think there is a kernel of hope in here, too.

MIDNIGHT SONATA

THADEUS TAPPED THE IVORY KEYS, IGNORING THE BLACK, each string struck and released to reverberate throughout the concert hall. Strike... release. Strike... release. Mechanical in its perfection, imperfect in its beauty; counterpoint to the chanting calls outside. He preferred modes arising from the equal-tempered scale. Though others gravitated to the Pythagorean with its mathematically precise intervals, he held to tradition—even to his choice of instrument. The venerable Bösendorfer 290 with its nine additional keys was the true star of his show. When asked why he insisted on playing an instrument five centuries old, he had no answer. With each stop on the tour, it required maintenance and tuning, but how could he even consider retiring such a work of art?

Chalk it up to the callowness of youth, he thought. At ninety-four, he was too young to have such a rigid opinion. Far more likely he inherited the preference—along with the instrument—from Christoph. The old man stopped playing years ago, when joints grew too stiff for what he called "an effective performance". Teaching became Christoph's art until the pain became too much to ignore. It wasn't the pain in his joints, but that in his heart as even his most modest students surpassed him. Thadeus was Christoph's last and greatest.

Thadeus lingered on a simple Phrygian cadence, ignoring the swelling sounds outside the hall, then shifted abruptly into A Minor. No altered scale degrees for harmonic or melodic tension—just pure minor in all its modal glory. Rapid arpeggios built in volume and tempo until he could take it no longer, and modulated into sparkling C♯ Major. The progression ran in thirds rather than staid fourth and fifths, denying traditional cadences. Melodic and harmonic tension leaked away, and Thadeus slowed the tempo in a long ritardando, finishing at last in C Major with simple triads at the edge of audible. The Bösendorfer happily obliged, strings vibrating in ever-decreasing amplitude. A rhythmic chant from protesters outside swelled to cover the last delicate notes.

Meaty clapping from a single pair of hands erupted behind, and he turned to the man leaning on an old-fashioned push-broom.

"Beautiful," the man said, grabbing the handle and moving closer. "You're gonna bring the house down with that one tomorrow night." He winked, then bent back to his work.

"It's not on the program," Thadeus demurred. "It's not finished, regardless."

The other straightened, then cocked his head. "Sounds finished to these ears."

"Thank you," Thadeus said, refusing to argue. *An early Wilson Sweeper model by the look of him.* A five or six series, their logic programming was rudimentary, but were built to last. One arm peeked from the short-sleeved coverall, darker than the rest of him—a past replacement.

The Wilson shuffled closer. "Yes, sir, you play real good," he said, cocking an eyebrow. "Thadeus model, right?"

"Yes. Thirty-seven series."

The other whistled, a long downward portamento. "Heard 'bout them. Supposed to be surgeons, right?"

"Yes," Thadeus nodded.

"Programming went all kerflooey, I hear." He edged closer to the piano bench. "Can't be more'n three or four of you left."

"I am the last," Thadeus said with sad pride.

The Wilson sat, still holding the handle of the broom. "Mind if I sit here a bit?"

Thadeus did mind, but not enough to complain. He scooted aside and nodded assent.

The Wilson touched a key, a soft brush of fingertips, like petting a massive beast. "Did you hear about Christoph?" he said without looking up.

"Yes. He was a teacher of mine." *That's not true*, Thadeus thought. *He was my only teacher.* There were others who could claim to have instructed the world's greatest pianist, but only one taught him anything of real value. To play with emotion, without letting emotion rule the music. A skill few humans ever mastered, and, until Thadeus, no machine.

The Wilson pressed middle C—a self-conscious, furtive motion. The note sounded a question in the cavernous space.

"I think it's sad humans die." He looked into Thadeus' eyes. "There are so few left."

"I don't know I would call two billion 'a few', but the numbers dwindle every year." Thadeus felt like crying, but couldn't. That ability was not part of his original design. Instead, he sighed. "Christoph was the last of his kind, you know."

The Wilson tilted his head, eyebrows meeting in the middle as he pondered. "I don't understand."

"He was the last living professional musician," Thadeus said with another sigh. "Humans won't commit the time required to perform at a professional level. Not since I came along at least. He finished with a sad shake of his head. "Now they build more just like me, and—"

"There are none like you, Thadeus," the Wilson said, his voice reverent.

Thadeus lowered his head. "That's because Christoph was the only human willing to give all his knowledge to a machine."

"There were no others?"

"Not with his genius." He lowered his forehead to the cool instrument, stretching his arms across, caressing it like a lover. "Now there are none," he whispered, stroking the lid, a great black sea of old-growth wood.

"One may come along, yet." He patted Thadeus on the back with a light touch. "You'll see." He stood, his hand resting there, then stepped away to return to his programmed task.

Thadeus straightened and watched the Wilson push his broom, then turned to the darkened house. *Maybe I could teach*, he thought. *Find a willing human, and...* But he knew better. Those days were gone, replaced by endless protests for jobs that would never return—replaced by his kind. He lifted his hands to the keyboard and wept for humanity's loss the only way he knew. Tentatively at first, but with growing resolve, he teased Beethoven's *Moonlight Sonata* from the instrument, the Wilson dancing his broom in time across the dark and empty stage.